Love, From the Fifth-Grade Celebrity

PATRICIA REILLY GIFF
Illustrated by LESLIE MORRILL

A YEARLING BOOK

Published by
Bantam Doubleday Dell Books for Young Readers
a division of
Bantam Doubleday Dell Publishing Group, Inc.
1540 Broadway
New York, New York 10036

ISBN: 0-440-44948-0

Reprinted by arrangement with Delacorte Press

Printed in the United States of America

One Previous Edition

August 1987

10 9

CWO

for Ge♡rge Nicholson

1

"Row, row, row your boat," Casey Valentine sang at the top of her lungs.

Her friend Tracy Matson opened her mouth wide, trying to drown her out. "Gently down the stream," she shouted.

Casey took a breath and swiped at her bangs. They were too long again. Stringy too. Her forehead was wet from the heat.

"Is that someone calling me?" she asked. She raised the rowboat oars a little. Drops of water rolled off the edges and plinked back into the river.

Everything was still. She looked down to see a school of silver fish streak by in the clear water.

Last day, she told herself, feeling a lump in her throat. Last day for the mountains and the river, last day with Tracy Matson.

She looked across at Tracy in the opposite end of the boat. Tracy's legs dangled over the side, her feet touching the water. Casey had to smile. Tracy's braids and freckles were the same color as Walter Moles's cat, Carrots.

"Watch out, Casey!" Tracy screeched. "We're going to crash."

"Watch out, Casey!" Tracy screeched.

Casey jumped. She clunked the oars into the water.

Too late. The rowboat hit the side of the bridge with a thump.

Casey looked at the slash of green paint on the bridge piling and ran her tongue over her braces. "Good grief! I hope nobody saw that." She glanced up.

Leroy Wilson was running back and forth on the bridge, pointing at them and making whooping noises.

"What's that goon doing?" Tracy asked.

"Making fun of us, I guess." Casey gave her bangs another swipe. "Let's get out of here."

"Idiot," Tracy yelled up at Leroy. "If you don't stop that, I'm going to come up there and knock your block off."

"Chickadee," Leroy yelled at her, laughing. "Slowest reading group in the world." He leaned over the bridge and tossed down a fish head. It hit the side of the boat with a smack.

Tracy stood up and started to scramble out on the rocks after him.

"Yeow," Casey yelled. "Get back in." She tried to steady the boat with the oars.

Leroy, still laughing, pounded down the bridge and disappeared up High Flats Road.

"Dummy," Tracy said, sliding down on the seat. "We'll get him later."

Casey nodded. "We'll think of a fantastic trick to play on him before I leave."

"Don't say it," Tracy said. "Don't even think about leaving. We still have an hour."

Casey dug the oars into the water and pushed away from the rocks. "We could put a crayfish on his bicycle seat."

"Really." Tracy grinned. "It would pinch him right in the—" She broke off. "Or we could get a couple of Mrs. Baxter's tomatoes, rotten ones. Stuff them in his sneaker toes while he's swimming."

Casey raised her face. She could almost feel her freckles popping out in the strong sun. "We could hang a sign from the bridge: Leroy Wilson Acts Like an Ape."

"Looks Like an Ape."

"A big sign," Casey said. "Leroy Wilson . . ."

"Is a Slob."

"Is he?"

"He rubs his hands in fish guts, then wipes them off on the bridge rail."

Casey shuddered. "Gross."

"He says it makes him a better fisherman," Tracy said. "That's why I never hold on to the railing anymore."

"I wish you had told me that sooner." Casey bent over the side of the boat and plunged her hands into the water. "Fine time to tell me on the morning I'm going home."

"Don't talk about going home," Tracy said.

Casey sighed. "This is the best vacation I ever had. I love High Flats."

Tracy leaned forward. "Me too. The vacation, I

mean." She grinned. "It was a little strange getting to know someone who wasn't from the country. You didn't even know how to row, remember?"

Casey crinkled her forehead under her bangs. "I may not be able to row so hot, but I can do a lot of other things."

They grinned at each other. "Don't mention my reading," Tracy said.

"It's a little better now." Casey looked down at the water. Tracy was the world's worst. She could hardly read *Peter Rabbit.*

"We'll write to each other," Tracy said, "even after school starts."

"Sure." Summer was almost over, Casey thought. She couldn't wait until school began. "Fifth grade is going to be spectacular," she said dreamily. "I'm going to try for class president. If I win, it will be two years in a row."

Tracy didn't answer.

"I'll be some kind of a celebrity with a record like that." She looked across at Tracy. Tracy was frowning. Maybe it was because she was a terrible reader. Maybe she hated school. Maybe she had never been elected class president. "Were you ever . . ." she began.

"Watch out for that big rock," Tracy said, pointing.

"I see it." Casey pushed hard on her left oar. "You know what else? Walter Moles's mother is going to have a baby in September. I can baby-sit whenever I want. She said so."

Tracy made a face. "I wouldn't want a baby next

door to me. It'll probably scream its head off. Nobody in the neighborhood will be able to sleep."

"I don't mind," Casey said. "I wish it were my mother instead of Mrs. Moles."

"What does Walter say?"

Casey pushed back her bangs again. "Who knows? He's probably too busy with his science stuff to think about a baby."

She sat there for a moment thinking about her friend Walter. What was the matter with him lately? Something was wrong. For the past few weeks before she left home he had looked as if he were sucking on lemons.

She felt a little worm of worry in her chest. She wondered if it was something she had done. She'd have to find out when she got home.

Just then Leroy yelled to them from the bridge.

"Don't pay any attention to him," Tracy said. "Really. He's up to something."

Casey looked back at the bridge.

"Your mother's looking all over the place for you, Casey Valentine," Leroy yelled. "The car's packed, the motor's running . . ."

"He's not fooling around," Casey said. She looked at Tracy. "It's been a great summer." She could feel a lump in her throat again.

Tracy looked as if she were going to cry. "Remember the rides at the fair?"

Casey nodded. "The day we went on the hayride?"

"The fish we caught?"

"The play we almost put on," Casey said. She sat there for another minute, then she dug the oars into the water and started to row for the landing.

2

D-liver
D-letter
D-sooner
D-better

Monday, August 12

Dear Tracy Matson,

Yes, it's me, the celebrity kid, Cassandra Eleanor Valentine. I told everyone about the week I spent in High Flats on vacation.

I told them about you too. Are your ears burning up?

Everyone here knows now that you're the best fisherperson in the country. They know, too, what a riot you are . . . that you and your neighbor Leroy Wilson are always playing tricks and driving each other crazy.

Sorry I haven't written sooner. Did you think I was kidnapped? Dead?

No, *ma chère*. I am alive and growing. Growing too fast. When I got home from vacation I noticed that I am taller than Walter Moles now. (I try to scrunch down whenever I see him.) He's really been cranky lately. I still don't know why.

Guess what? A celebrity author came to the library yesterday. She had four earrings in each ear and a fake gold nail on her pinky finger.

She gets to go all over the country and meet famous people like Judy Blume.

I have definitely decided to be a writer too. The celebrity kind.

I'm going to write a wonderful book . . . an exciting book. I'll send you some parts when I get going.

Write back soon.

Love,
Casey

3

Monday, August 19

Dear Casey,

I told everyone in High Flats you are writeing a book, the real kind that will probly get published.

At first that fink Leroy Wilson didn't believe me, but now he does. We are going into ~~busnus~~ biznis together.

Guess what kind?

We are going to ~~see~~ sell your book. We made this stand and everything. Mrs. Wilson said we can put her down for too copies. Also Mrs. Clausson will probly by too to. too too.

If you can tell me how soon the book will be ready. A weak maybe?

Everybudy is wateing. Reely.

Love,
Tracy

P.S. Poopsie Pomerantz wanted to be in the ~~busnus~~ biznis too. But she spraned her arm again. I'm the one who got blamed for everything. We were riding down High Flats Road, looking for wood for the stand. I saw a new sign. "Watch out," I screemed to Poopsie. "It's a bomb."

Poopsie through herself off the bike. She landed on a rock.

Leroy was laughing his fool head off.

He said the sign only said BUMP.

(Mrs. Pomerantz isn't laughing. She's mad¢ as a hen. She says she thinks my mother should send me to bording school.)

P.S. Again. I may have some exiding news for you. Keep your toes crossed.

XXXXXOOOOO

4

Dear Amanda Cornfield,

I had a great time when you came to our library. I really love your books.

I'm writing a book too. I figure it has to be exciting, scary, horrible, and sad . . . all at the same time.

I've been working on it for two weeks, but it's not coming out right. In fact, it's not coming out at all.

Can you tell me how to get started?

I am enclosing a stamped self-addressed envelope. Please send an answer. I need to know right away, or *tout de suite* as they say in French.

Yours till Niagara Falls,
and the kitchen sinks, (ha)
Cassandra Eleanor Valentine

5

August 24

Dear Casey,

I have bad news and good news.

First the bad. I can't sell youre book for a wile.

The reeson why is the good news. My mother has lost her job. My father is in between jobs too. He's going to help build a house with my uncle Gerry.

Guess where?

In the next town from you. We are going to stay at Uncle Gerry's apartment. It's right near you.

I'll be able to go to school with you and see you every day for a wile. (Leroy Wilson is going to take care of my dog, Rebel. I am going to pay him too old fising rods and forty-eight cents.)

See you in a few days. Tell everybudy it's reely going to be a slam bang time.

Love ya,
Tracy

〜orry

) o

) loppy

P.S. Poopsie Pomerantz is not the only one with a spraned ankel. I have a broken rist. It was not a bomb this time.

This time I was working on the stand. (You know the one for your book. What's it about by-the-way?)

Anyway I figerd the stand should be bigger. Peple around here will be very excided when they find out they know a real celebridy riter.

I tried to stick some more bords onto the end of the stand, but I hammad my rist with the hamma.

Now I have a cast. That bone head Leroy Wilson made his name as big as a crokodile rite on the front.

I was mad as hops.

P.S. again. Poopsie Pomeranz rote this for me. I did the spelling part because she's not to good at it.

"I was working on the stand."

6

Casey pressed her nose against the screen. She tried to ignore the scratchy feeling in her throat.

"Half the afternoon is gone and the mailman still hasn't come," she said over her shoulder to her sister, Van. "I've been waiting forever for a letter from Amanda Cornfield."

"Who?"

"You know, the famous author."

Van didn't answer. She was standing on her head in the middle of the black and yellow bedroom rug. "Twelve Mississippi, thirteen Mississippi."

"Vannie? Answer me."

Van flopped over on her stomach. "What a pain you are, Casey. I'm trying to practice. If I ever get to be the world's greatest gymnast, it'll be a miracle with you hanging around, bothering me all the time."

"Don't worry. I'm leaving right now." Casey started down the stairs, shoving her birthday money in her jeans pocket. "Today's the day Tracy Matson's coming," she called over her shoulder.

"And tomorrow . . . one Mississippi . . . is the first day . . . two Mississippi . . . of school," Van said.

Casey opened the front door, raced across the lawn, and banged on Walter's front door.

Walter's grandmother, Mrs. Thorrien, poked her head out. *"Bonjour,"* she said. "How goes my little French student this day?"

Casey grinned at her. *"Bien.* I think I know thirty words now."

"Très bien. I will think of some more for you."

"I want to learn a whole pile." Casey looked toward the driveway. "Is Walter around?"

Mrs. Thorrien shook her head. "He was up in the bathroom, but now he's gone. The bathroom is"—she shook her head—"is feelthy. Water in the tub. Water on the floor." She frowned. "Footprints."

Casey took a step backwards. Walter was never around anymore. "Tell him I was here when you see him. I have to run. I'm on my way over to 204th Street. My friend Tracy Matson should be there by now."

Mrs. Thorrien nodded. "That is happy news, Casey. I'll tell Waltair . . ."

Casey didn't wait for Mrs. Thorrien to finish. She raced up the block and darted across the street.

She was dying to see Tracy. What a time they were going to have.

She turned the corner. Halfway up the street she spotted Mr. Matson's old green pickup truck parked next to the curb. Mr. and Mrs. Matson were nowhere in sight, but Tracy was standing up in the back slinging boxes out onto the street.

"Hey, Tracy," Casey shouted.

Tracy shaded her eyes with her hand. "Is that you, Casey Valentine?" She jumped off the truck and wiped her hands against her cutoff jeans.

For a moment Casey stood there staring at her. Tracy's freckles, the red braids that were half undone, even the ripped shorts and the shirt were the same.

But Tracy looked different away from High Flats and the boat and the river. It wasn't the grayish cast on her arm either.

Tracy started toward her. Then Casey started to run too. They grabbed each other in a bear hug.

"You look different," Tracy told her.

"I was thinking the same thing about you," Casey said.

They both laughed. "Now you look right," Casey said.

"Glad you didn't bring half the world with you," Tracy said after a moment. "Your friends or something. I look like Mr. Baxter's prize sow. A real oink." She spit on her finger and rubbed at a spot on her shirt. "My father and Uncle Gerry went over to the new house, my mother's unpacking our stuff." She held the bottom of the shirt out. "Ruined, I guess." She shook her head. "The trip was so long I thought we'd hit China any minute."

"You look great," Casey said. "Never mind your shirt."

"And how about this cast?" Tracy stuck her arm out. "It's not everyone who gets to wear one of these."

Casey banged her knuckles against it. "Right." She picked up a red plaid suitcase. "I'll help."

They made three trips into the apartment building, lugging boxes and shopping bags and scratched-up suitcases.

Mrs. Matson, her head tied in a pink checked scarf, gave Casey a quick kiss and patted Tracy on the shoulder. "You've grown," she said to Casey. She hurried back and forth from the kitchen to the living room trying to open all the boxes at once.

Mrs. Matson looked different away from High Flats, too, Casey thought. It was probably the scarf, or maybe it was because she was wearing a dress.

"Get lost," Mrs. Matson told them finally. "I'll finish up."

Tracy stuck her head under the faucet in the sink and slurped up some water. She bumped her head standing up. "Good grief, I forgot about your book. Here I am talking like an idiot when the main thing . . ."

Casey ran her tongue over her braces. "It's not exactly fin—"

"Coming along just great, I'll bet. We'll probably sell a million copies. Maybe more. We'll end up rich as a bank."

Casey swallowed. Her throat felt sore. "I guess so." She tried to think of something else to talk about. She didn't want to think about the four miserable pages she had written, most of them scratched out and erased.

"Listen, Mom," Tracy said. "We'll be back soon.

I've got to send a postcard to Leroy Wilson right
away. I want to remind him about taking care of
Rebel—dog food and all that stuff." She took a breath.
"I may even send a card to Rebel." She wiggled her
nose at Casey. "See if he can recognize my scent."

"Tommy's Ten-Cent Store has cards," Casey said.
"Sodas too." She patted her pocket. "I've got
money."

They walked down the street toward Hollis Avenue, Casey counting off on her fingers as she told
Tracy about the kids in the class. "There's Mindy,"
she said, "out of it, but nice. And Catherine Wilson,
smart. Darlene, a leader type . . ."

"Like you," Tracy said. "You were president of
your class last year, weren't you?"

"You remembered that?" Casey said, pleased.
"Maybe this year too."

"You might not have time with all this writing every minute."

"Don't worry. I'll—" She broke off. "Hey, is that
Walter up there? Turning into the ten-cent store?"
She cupped her hands around her mouth. "Wa-a-al-
ter-r-r!"

Walter didn't look up. He opened the door to the
store and disappeared inside.

"Come on," Casey said. "We'll get him a soda too."
She swallowed. Her throat was getting scratchier every minute, and her stomach wasn't right either.

A moment later they turned in at the ten-cent
store. Casey took a deep breath. It smelled like old
socks and chocolate candy. Her stomach lurched.

"What's the matter?" Tracy asked.

Casey shook her head. "Nothing, I guess. Felt sick for a minute." She craned her neck. "There's Walter, over in the hardware section."

They went closer. "Hi, Walter," Tracy said. "Remember me from last summer?"

"Sure I remember. We were in High Flats for a week." He began to paw through a bunch of tan corks. He picked up a cork, pushed his glasses higher on his nose, and squinted at it.

"What's that for?" Casey asked.

"Science experiment," he said. He gave a quarter to the woman behind the counter.

"Want a bag?" she asked.

Walter shook his head. He shoved the cork in his pocket.

"How about a soda?" Casey asked. "Chocolate maybe? Or lemon?" Her stomach gave another heave.

Walter shook his head. "Busy." He sounded grumpy. "I'm right in the middle of everything. The bathroom's a disaster. If my grandmother gets a look at it"—he drew his finger across his neck—"curtains." He hurried up the aisle and out the door.

Casey stared after him.

"What's the matter with him?" Tracy asked.

Casey shook her head. "I don't know. He's usually more fun than anyone else." She smiled at Tracy. "Except for you, of course."

"Really." Tracy grinned.

Casey swallowed. She felt terrible. She wished she were home in bed. She could almost feel the coolness of the sheets. She tried not to think about it. "Walter's been acting like this for a couple of weeks. Ever since . . ." She thought for a moment. "I can't remember."

"How about that soda?" Tracy asked.

Casey swallowed. "I think my stomach . . ." she began. "Maybe a virus. My throat hurts too."

"You look a little green," Tracy said. "Maybe you should go home."

"Maybe." Casey reached into her pocket and pulled out a dollar. "Here, better have that soda on your own."

She hurried up the aisle, waving back at Tracy, who was still standing there, the money in her outstretched hand. "Sorry. I'm really sorry."

"Hey, Casey," Tracy called after her. "Wait a minute."

Casey looked back.

"Don't say anything . . . about my reading, you know? I don't want everyone to think . . ."

Casey waved her hand. "Don't worry." She headed along Hollis Avenue for home, crossing in front of the mailman. At last he was getting around to 200th Street.

She didn't even wait to find out whether Amanda Cornfield had finally written to her. She felt sick, really sick. She hoped she'd be all right by tomorrow.

She had to be all right. It would be terrible to miss the first day of school.

She went straight upstairs and dived into bed.

7

"What a bomb," Casey muttered the next afternoon. She ripped the first four pages out of her notebook and tore them into tiny bits. Start over, she told herself.

She punched the pillows into shape, took a sip of the lemonade her mother had brought up a few minutes ago, then began to print carefully. DYING DAYS, by Cassandra Eleanor Valentine.

She lay back against the pillows and fluttered her eyelids. "Dying," she whispered to herself. "Yes, excellent title."

She sat up a little higher and wrote the first few sentences.

A few minutes later the screen door banged open downstairs.

"Is that you, Van?" she yelled. She shoved the notebook under the pillows as Van burst into the room.

"Hey, Casey, out of my bed." Van dumped a pile of books on the bottom of the yellow spread.

"Come on, Vanny. My bed's full of Ritz cracker crumbs."

"Out."

Casey slid out of bed onto the floor. "Pizza face." Van flopped across her bed. "I'm wiped out. Ex-

"Dying," Casey whispered to herself.

hausted. You wouldn't understand. Junior high is very different from the Ogden School."

"Big deal, Lucille." Casey pressed on her stomach to see if it still hurt.

Van sat up. "You've got dots of paper all over my bed. Cracker crumbs too."

Casey giggled. " 'Somebody's been eating in my bed,' said the baby bear."

"Not funny," Van said. "What is this stuff, anyway? It's not Ritz."

"Who knows?" Casey said. "Maybe Social Teas. Vanilla wafers."

"I thought you were sick."

"I'm better." Casey swallowed. Her throat didn't hurt much anymore. She frowned. "I told Mother I didn't have to stay home from school today."

Van brushed at the sheet, then pulled at the books on the bottom of the bed. "Look at these. Heavy as lead. Seventh grade is going to be tough. Very tough."

"Can I borrow some of that plum raisin polish?" Casey went over to Van's dresser and looked at the nail polish bottles. "My luck to miss the first day of school. Tracy was counting on me to show her around, introduce her to everyone."

"Hey, what's this?" Van said from the bed. She began to laugh.

Casey looked up. "What?"

"This." Van waved the blue notebook around in the air.

"Give me that, worm face. It's mine."

Van stood up on her bed. "DYING DAYS," she shouted.

Casey climbed on the bed after her. "I'm going to kill you, Van."

"Michelle Vandervine fluttered her beautiful eyelashes up and down," Van read in a loud voice.

"I hate you." Casey slid down on the bed. "I really detest . . ."

"Michelle Vandervine had Black River plague." Van looked up. "What's that?"

Casey shrugged, embarrassed. "A disease. I just made it up."

Van tossed the notebook over to her, still laughing. "What's this supposed to be anyway, a book?"

"None of your airhead business." She kicked the notebook under her bed, then spotted last year's green assignment pad on top of Van's books. "Hey. What are you doing with this? How come you have to get into all my private stuff?"

"Walter told me to give it to you. I'm surprised you'd let anyone look through that mess."

"I didn't," Casey said. "I just threw it out the window to him this morning. I didn't have time to get a new one." She shook her head. "Walter wouldn't read it, anyway. He was just going to copy my homework assignment for me." She flipped through the pages. Walter had written:

CMPO—Mp Suumir Vooteon.

She wondered what it meant.

Van stuck her face up against the mirror. "Gonna get my hair cut. Long on top, tapered in the back.

It'll make me look more like a junior high school kid instead of a nerdy little ex-sixth grader."

"I don't know how Walter gets away with handwriting like this." She glanced at Van. "Nothing's wrong with your hair."

Van made a face. "It looks like a bunch of weeds. Dead weeds." She pulled her purse out from under her books. "I've got to go to the library. By the way, I saw Tracy Matson."

"Poor kid," Casey said. "I'll bet she had a terrible day without me."

"I don't think so. She was walking home with Darlene and Catherine, laughing and fooling around. She said she had a wild time in the lunchroom, telling everyone how she taught you to row."

Casey frowned a little. "I thought she'd be shy . . . nervous . . ." Her voice trailed off.

"I guess not." Van opened the bedroom door and started down the stairs, her voice floating back. "She said she told them about your slamming into every rock in the whole river . . . said the bridge is hanging by a thread . . . next year you'll probably knock it down . . ."

Casey puffed out her cheeks and blew through her braces. "Tracy said that? She told that on me?" She stamped over to the window in time to see Van start across the front lawn. "What else did she say?" she called down.

Van glanced up, shading her eyes. "She's coming over to see if you're still alive."

"Right now?"

"In a little while." Van waved her hand and disappeared around the corner.

Casey looked over at Walter's lawn. Carrots, his cat, was pretending to stalk a squirrel. He was too fat to catch even a turtle. Mrs. Moles, Walter's mother, was sitting in a lounge chair.

"Do you know where Walter is?" Casey called down. "I want to ask him about the homework."

Mrs. Moles looked up. "In the bathroom, I think. He's working on some science thing. The tub's full of water again. Last night it sloshed over the side."

"Would you tell him I'm looking for him? When you go in, I mean?"

"Sure, Casey. I have to get up in a minute."

"How are you anyway?"

"A couple of days. Maybe next week. Who knows?"

Lucky Walter, Casey thought. A new baby any day. She turned away from the window, slid down on the floor, and stared at Walter's writing in her assignment pad.

Everything had started in fifth grade. Too bad she didn't know one thing that was going on.

8

Casey looked around the bedroom. It was a disaster. Blankets on the floor, sheets full of cracker crumbs, a bunch of shorts and shirts draped over the desk.

So what, she thought. Tracy Matson was pretty much of a mess too. She knelt up and looked out the window again to see if Tracy was on her way.

Yes, she was halfway up the block, her carroty braids bouncing. Casey drew in her breath. Darlene and Catherine, and even Mindy, were right behind her.

Good grief, she thought. Darlene's bedroom looked like a movie star's.

Quickly she kicked the blankets and sheets under her bed, tossed Van's yellow spread on top, and gathered up the pile of clothes in her arms.

She heard the bell ring, and then her mother's voice. "Some of the kids are here, Casey. I'm sending them up."

Casey dumped the clothes on her closet floor and slid into bed.

Tracy banged open the door. "We're here to cheer you up, Casey old girl."

The others crowded in in back of Tracy. Darlene was wearing knickers and pink spangled socks. That

Darlene had everything. Bracelets too. Casey counted. Four of them. Two pinks, a yellow, and a purple.

Real celebrity stuff.

If only she could get her book written. What a celebrity thing that would be.

"Aren't you going to ask us to sit down?" Catherine asked, giggling.

Catherine was always giggling. Casey cleared her throat, thinking that there was really no place for them to sit. The only chair was a midget one she had gotten on her fifth birthday. It collapsed every time someone went near it. Too bad she didn't have a couple of chairs like Darlene's. Poufy things.

She waved her hand. "Sit on Van's bed, *mes chères.*"

Darlene and Catherine perched on the edge, but Tracy plumped herself down on Van's pillow.

"I can sit on the floor, I guess," Mindy said. She sank down at the bottom of Casey's bed. Casey could just about see the top of her head.

"Big news," Tracy said. "Everything got going to-day."

Darlene pulled at the ends of her dark hair, curling them around her finger. "Homework already. A composition on My Summer Vacation. Same thing every year." She looked at Tracy. "But one thing's new. The greatest kid."

"Ta da," Tracy said. "That's me."

"Summer vacation," Casey repeated. "I should

have known." She pictured Walter's handwriting scrawled across her assignment pad: suumir vooteon.

"What's this notebook?" Mindy asked.

"It will be an easy composition for you, Casey," Tracy said at the same time. "You can tell about coming to High Flats on vacation and about how you learned to row." She twirled her braids over her head. "Ta da," she said again. "Make sure you give me credit."

Darlene and Catherine began to laugh. "That was the funniest story," Catherine said, "about Casey dropping the oars into the river, bumping into everything . . ."

"Like a little elephant," Tracy said, grinning.

Casey frowned and turned to Darlene. "When are we going to vote for class president?"

"How sad," Mindy said.

"Sad? Voting?" Darlene asked.

"No, I didn't mean that," Mindy began. "I meant . . ."

"Out of it," Darlene said.

"Tell us about Leroy Wilson, Tracy," Catherine cut in. "Tell us about one of your famous tricks."

Tracy bounced on the bed. "Well. Last week Leroy was trying to fish. I told him he was doing it all wrong. Really. He kept leaning over the bridge, tangling up his line. I figured I'd give him a good scare. I snuck down . . ."

"When are we going to vote?" Casey asked as Tracy stopped to take a breath.

"We did vote," Darlene said.

"Shh," said Catherine. "Let's hear the end of the story."

"I got under the bridge," Tracy went on, "grabbed Leroy's fishing line, and gave it a tremendous tug. That idiot boy thought he had a whale or something on the hook. Then I screamed 'Shark!' Leroy went screeching down the bridge."

"You are the funniest," Catherine said, laughing. "I bet the kids in High Flats miss you."

"Well . . ." Tracy said.

"Who's Michelle?" Mindy cut in.

"What about that crazy assignment?" Darlene said. She rattled the bracelets on her arm.

"Really," said Tracy.

"Tell me everything, *mes chères,*" Casey said. "Tell me about the voting first, though."

Tracy grinned at her. "Don't you want that part for a surprise?"

Casey could feel her heart speed up. She nodded a little. She bet she had been elected. Probably everyone was here to tell her.

"Then we'll tell the voting part last," Tracy said. She slid down a little farther on the bed.

"Yes, start at the beginning," said Catherine.

"The beginning is the new teacher," Darlene said. "Her name is Mrs. Eddie. She's tall, skinny, nice . . . laughs kind of like a horse . . ."

"A little absentminded," Catherine cut in.

"She says we're going to read a lot," Darlene said. "Tons of books."

Casey glanced at Tracy. She wondered how she'd feel about doing a pile of reading.

Tracy's face did look a little red. She began to talk fast. "Now it's time to tell about the assignment. You and me are partners, Casey old girl."

"Let me tell," Darlene said. She pushed back her hair, rattling her bracelets again. "We're going to have a play kind of thing with skits. It'll be in the middle of September. We have to choose someone famous. Learn all about the person. Dress up like . . ."

"We can pick anyone we like?" Someone fantastic, Casey thought. A celebrity kind of person. Someone different, like . . . maybe Sally Ride, the astronaut, or Geraldine Ferraro.

"I thought we'd pick someone easy," Tracy said. "I put us down for George Washington."

"George Washington?" Casey repeated. "You've got to be kidding."

"We're picking someone really cool," Darlene said. "Catherine and I."

"Father of our country," said Tracy. "Stuff like that."

"We'll look like a pair of babies," Casey said. "Everyone learns all that in kindergarten."

"We'll work out the details later," Tracy said, reaching under her cast to scratch. "Itchy as anything."

Casey took a breath. "I'm not doing George . . ."

"Don't you want to hear about class president?" Tracy asked.

Casey nodded.

"Dying," Mindy said in a sad voice.

Tracy scratched at her arm again. "Three out of five people in this room have been elected to important things in the classroom."

"Yes?" Casey asked, feeling a little sorry for Tracy. Mindy too. Mindy never got elected to anything.

"I'm the secretary," Darlene said. "I'm going to take care of all the writing-down stuff—records, you know."

"And I'm the vice president," Catherine said.

Casey sat up a little in bed.

"Ta da!" Tracy twirled her braids around. "Guess who's the president?"

"Well . . ." Casey began.

"Tracy Matson herself," Tracy said. "And it's really all because of you."

Casey swallowed. "Because of me?"

"Telling everyone about High Flats. Telling everyone about me and my tricks. All those funny things. Really."

Casey stared at her. Tracy was grinning all over the place like a big baboon. "You're the president? You?" Just then she heard a voice yelling outside. "That's Walter," she said.

Tracy bounced up from the bed. "Let me." She poked her head against the window screen. "Casey's in bed. She's too sick to come out."

"No, I'm not." Casey slid out of the bed and went to the window.

"Listen," Darlene said. "It's time for us to go anyway."

Casey looked back over her shoulder. "See you tomorrow." She tried to smile at them. "Thanks for coming."

"Just tell me, Casey," Mindy said, "about Michelle Vander—whatever her name is. She's dying of the plague?"

"Plague?" Catherine echoed. "That could wipe out a whole country."

Casey stared at them, and then at the notebook in Mindy's hand, wondering how Mindy had gotten her hands on it.

"What's that anyway?" Darlene asked, reaching for the notebook.

"Is that the story you're writing?" Tracy asked.

Darlene tossed the notebook on the bed. "Couldn't be. It's real baby stuff."

"Right," Casey said. "From second grade or something like that."

But no one was listening to her. They were laughing at Tracy, who had thrown herself on the floor pretending she was dead.

"Come on, Tracy," Darlene said. "I can't bear to walk home alone."

Tracy scrambled up. "You're in luck. I'm on my way."

Casey turned back to the window and looked down at Walter as the girls started for the stairs. Walter's hands were stained with something blue. "What are you doing?" she asked.

"Nothing much." He rubbed his hands on his jeans.

She listened to the girls banging out the front door. "How was school?"

"Terrible." He nodded at the girls as they passed him, then looked up at her again. "I guess you're glad Tracy's here."

Casey pressed her nose against the screen.

She could see Tracy prancing down the street, taking a little skip every few steps. The other three girls were listening, faces turned toward her.

Casey sighed. She should be glad that Tracy was president. Glad that the kids thought she was so great. After all, she was her best friend outside of Walter.

She watched, waiting to see if anyone would turn to wave. When they turned the corner, still talking, she looked back at Walter. She wondered if anyone had nominated her for class president. "Sure I'm glad," she told Walter after a moment. "Sure."

"That's what I thought. Get the assignment all right?"

Casey nodded. "Thanks. I'm going back to bed for a while."

She sat down on the edge of the bed and scooped up the notebook. Then she took a pencil and crossed out the page in heavy dark lines.

9

The next morning Casey stepped over Walter's cat, Carrots, and hurried down her front path. She caught up with Walter at the corner. He was twirling a leaf around in his hands. His fingers still had blotches of blue on them.

"What's that stuff anyway?" Casey asked.

"Nothing." He held up the leaf. "Look, the first one. It's getting orange around the edges."

"About time," she said. "I'm sick of the hot weather. I can't wait for a little snow and—" She broke off. "By that time your baby will be months old. Your mother said I can baby-sit whenever I want."

"That's all anyone thinks about," Walter said. "The baby."

"Won't it be great?"

Walter tore the leaf in half. "My grandmother's throwing a pile of my stuff away. She says we have to make room for it."

Casey stared at him. "You're a little grumpy lately, you know."

He tossed the leaf away. "Things on my mind."

She looked up at the trees, watching a squirrel dart from one branch to the next. She felt like telling him

"Things on my mind," Walter said.

that she had things on her mind too. Up until yesterday she thought she'd be class president.

"Hey," she said. "Just wondering. Did anyone think to nominate me for president?"

Walter raised one shoulder. "You wanted to be president again? Sorry, I was out of the classroom for the whole thing. Got a drink, then looked out the window."

She waved her hand. "Not important."

"I would have . . ."

She shook her head. Don't think about it, she told herself. Think about the book. She had started a new one last night, a tremendous book. It was going to be a mystery, *Summer Suspense.* There'd be a maniac-type killer in it. That was the best kind. She squinted up at the squirrel and grinned a little. Maybe she'd make the killer a kid, a kid with red braids and freckles, like Tracy's.

She shook her head. Terrible. It wasn't Tracy's fault that she had been elected president. She bent over and picked up a leaf too. If only she had been in school yesterday.

They turned in at the schoolyard gate and climbed the stairs to room 202. Casey jumped out of the way as Gunther Reed charged up ahead of them, then she and Walter followed him into the classroom.

It was still early. A group of kids were in the back, laughing over something. Casey craned her neck. She could see Tracy in the middle, her head bobbing up and down.

Mrs. Eddie was sitting at her desk, working. Casey went over to her, her absence note in her hand.

"Feeling better?" the teacher asked.

Casey nodded.

"You're the girl who likes to write."

"How did you know?"

"The girl from the country . . . lovely girl, class president already." She paused. "What's her name—Tracy—told me you were writing a book." Mrs. Eddie opened a black-and-white notebook. "She said it was almost finished, that it was going to be just wonderful."

"Almost finished?" Casey repeated.

"Yes," said Mrs. Eddie. "I think it would be lovely to read a little of it on the day we have the skits. Up on the stage."

"I'm not quite . . ." Casey began.

"Plenty of time to polish it up."

Casey gulped. "Where should I sit?"

Mrs. Eddie looked around and clapped her hands. "Be seated everyone. I want to look for an empty desk." She waited for a moment while everyone scrambled into place. "I want to start work in a minute too. We'll get some reading in first thing."

Casey looked around. There were two or three empty seats, one right in front of Gunther Reed.

She crossed her fingers.

"There." Mrs. Eddie pointed. "In front of that good-looking kid who doesn't comb his hair."

Gunther turned red and ducked his head.

Casey ducked her head too. She didn't want everyone to know that she thought Gooney was the cutest boy in the class—next to Walter, of course.

Mrs. Eddie nodded. "Yes, across from Tracy. She'll be your partner on the class project."

Casey walked down the aisle, slid into the empty seat, and shoved her looseleaf book into the desk.

Next to her Tracy was grinning.

She smiled back. She'd have to talk to Tracy about that skit business. She wasn't going to do George Washington. She shuddered when she even thought about it.

She'd have to talk to her about this writing business too. It was ridiculous for the whole world to know about her book when she didn't even have the first page finished.

She ran her tongue over her braces. She'd hate Tracy to know she didn't even have ten words stuck together yet.

Mrs. Eddie clapped her hands. "Let me tell you about reading. We're not going to use readers this year, just interesting books. I've ordered a pile of them."

Casey looked over at Tracy. She had her head in her desk, looking for something.

"We'll work in groups," said Mrs. Eddie. "We'll start with the first two rows. Bring up your chairs." She waved her hand. "The rest of you can work out the math examples I've written on the blackboard."

Casey stood up and dragged her chair to the front of the room, then looked back. Tracy's head was still buried in her desk.

Maybe she wasn't looking for anything, Casey thought. She was probably afraid the whole class was going to find out what a terrible reader she was.

Casey thought back to the day she had found out about Tracy's reading. All the kids in High Flats were putting on a play, and Tracy couldn't read her part.

Richard and Leroy were always calling her a chickadee, flapping their hands and making chirping noises. "Slowest reading group in the world," Leroy would say, and "Tracy is the slowest reader in the group," Richard would answer.

Poor Tracy, Casey thought, wondering how she'd feel if everyone in the fifth grade found out. Catherine, the smartest. Darlene, who had read fat mystery books even in first grade. Walter wouldn't care one bit, but Gooney would. He'd probably call Tracy Donkey Ears or something like that.

She looked back until at last Tracy pulled her head out from under her desk, her red braids looking sloppier than ever, and pulled her chair up next to Casey's.

Her cheeks were red, almost as red as her freckles. She smiled a little at Casey as Mrs. Eddie handed out books, but she looked as if she were going to cry.

Casey looked down quickly at her paperback. A mystery: *Summer of Suspense*. She couldn't believe it, almost the title of her own book. She opened it and began to read. The whole thing sounded familiar. Suddenly she remembered. She had read it in July.

It was much better than anything she could write.

She'd have to find another title, another story for her own book.

"We'll start with our class president," said Mrs. Eddie. "Would you read the first page, Tracy?"

It seemed a long time before Tracy began. She was holding the book in both hands, staring down at the cover.

"Summer," said Tracy. "Summer suspenders."

For a moment there was silence. Then everyone began to laugh.

"I can see why the class wanted you for president," Mrs. Eddie said, smiling. "You have a wonderful sense of humor."

Tracy bobbed her head a little, still looking down at her book. Then she glanced up at Mrs. Eddie. "I'm getting a sore throat. Maybe I caught Casey's virus."

"Want to get a drink?" Mrs. Eddie asked.

Tracy nodded. She pushed back her chair and threaded her way around the other kids.

"How about you, Casey," Mrs. Eddie asked.

Casey waited until the door closed behind Tracy. Then she opened to the first page.

"Summer of Suspense," she said. She cleared her throat and began to read.

10

On Friday Casey was later than usual arriving at the cafeteria. Half the class was there ahead of her. She picked up her hot lunch tray and sat down on the fifth-grade bench next to Darlene. Walter was sitting across the way.

She leaned forward. "How's your mother?"

Walter raised one shoulder.

"I can't wait for the baby," she said. "Your mother said I could walk her in the carriage."

She watched Walter frowning for a moment, then she looked down at her plate. The cafeteria helper had dumped chopped meat and beans on one side of it and a scoop of mashed potatoes—the instant kind —on the other. Friday was the worst hot-lunch day. She made a little road through the potatoes so the river of gravy could run out, then picked up her fork.

At that moment Tracy careened across the room. She shoved her tray on the table between Darlene's and Casey's and pushed herself between the two of them.

"Youch," Casey said. She took a lump of meat into her mouth. It tasted like pencil sharpener shavings.

"Reminds me of the dog food lunches we have at

the Thaddeus Lowell School in High Flats," Tracy said. She speared a piece of meat.

"Tell us another story about High Flats," Darlene said.

Tracy started in. "Casey will remember this. We really played some great tricks on old Leroy Wilson."

She waved her arm with the cast around, pushing Casey toward the end of the bench. Then she started to talk, going from one story to another, telling them about Leroy and how she had taught Casey to row a boat.

Casey thought back to her vacation in High Flats. It had been such a wonderful time, but it seemed so long ago now.

Tracy nudged her. She had a smear of gravy on the end of the cast. "Your class president taught you everything about the country, right? You didn't even know how to row a boat, or fish."

"I don't remember," Casey answered.

Mindy was the last one to sit. She slid onto the edge of the bench next to Walter, balancing her tray with both hands and holding a book under her arm.

She lost her balance for a moment and the book bounced off Walter's arm.

"Sorry," she said. "It's my Princess Di book."

Casey looked up. "What's that for?"

"The skit," Mindy said. "Joanne and I are doing her. Joanne has this marvelous hat, just like . . ."

Casey looked down at her plate. The gravy had hardened into an ice-skating rink. Princess Di, she thought. Even Mindy was doing someone better than George Washington.

She turned to Tracy. "Listen, Tracy. We've got to talk about this skit business."

Tracy waved her cast. "Nothing to talk about. We don't even have to practice. We can get up there, tell about old George, and be on our way. Nothing to it."

"I'm not doing it," Casey said.

Tracy tapped her arm with the cast. "Sure you are," she said, and grinned. "You have to do what your president tells you." She turned to Darlene. "I just thought of another story."

Casey picked up her tray and slid off the end of the bench.

Nobody even noticed she was gone. Too bad, she thought. She didn't care one bit. She looked back over her shoulder as she dumped the tray on the rack. Tracy was still talking about High Flats.

She'd go to Mrs. Eddie and find out if she could do her own skit.

Let Tracy do George Washington by herself.

Casey would choose someone else, someone really great.

She hurried upstairs to room 202, but Mrs. Eddie wasn't there. She was probably in the teachers' room.

Casey went downstairs again and knocked on the door. Mrs. Petty, her old fourth-grade teacher, opened it. She had a little rim of mashed potatoes on her upper lip.

"What's the problem, Cassandra?"

Casey leaned back. Mrs. Petty always spit when she said her *s*'s. "I'm looking for Mrs. Eddie."

"She's having something to eat," Mrs. Petty said. "Is it important? Can it wait? Can't she have a little peace during . . ."

Just then Mrs. Eddie spotted Casey. She came to the door with a book in her hand.

"Listen, Mrs. Eddie. I need to talk to you," Casey said.

Mrs. Eddie stepped outside.

"I was thinking," Casey began, wondering how she was going to say it. "About the skit."

"Yes?"

"I was thinking about doing it on my own."

Mrs. Eddie closed her book. "Who's your partner?"

"Tracy Matson."

"She's a lovely girl," Mrs. Eddie said, nodding.

"Yes."

"What's the problem, then, Casey?"

Casey tried to think of what to say. "No problem. I just want to do the skit alone."

Mrs. Eddie looked at Casey a little impatiently. "Go on."

"I have some ideas," Casey said slowly. "They won't work with two people."

Mrs. Eddie raised her eyebrows. "Half of this assignment is to teach people to work together. It's a team effort, you know?" She leaned a little closer. "And after all, you have the honor of reading your very own book on the stage."

Casey gulped. "But I was just thinking . . ."

"Why don't you think about working in pairs? Two by two, like the ark. Noah's ark." Mrs. Eddie smiled at her.

"But . . ." Casey began again.

"Listen, Casey, I'm starving. I want to sit down for two minutes, eat my lunch like the rest of the world, and read my book." She patted Casey on the shoulder and opened the door to the teachers' room. "How's your book coming, by the way?"

Casey gulped. "It's fine, I guess. Great."

"That's lovely."

"Yes," Casey said, as the door closed behind Mrs. Eddie. She went down the hall desperately trying to think of something to write about.

Too bad she didn't have the plague like poor old Michelle Vander—whatever her name was, she thought. She waited at the stairway for the bell to ring.

11

Casey let herself in the back door and dropped her books on the kitchen counter. Her mother was sitting at the table, hunched over a crossword puzzle. "How was school?"

"Not bad for a Monday," Casey said, and swallowed.

"It's hard getting back into the swing of things," her mother said. "I remember." She tapped her pencil against her teeth. "I wish I could remember the name of that movie star, the one who played in *On the Waterfront*. It has six letters."

Casey shook her head. "Do we have anything to eat?"

"No, I'm saving money this week."

Casey smiled a little. "Come on."

"Apple turnovers from yesterday—a little hard, but the apples are good. . . . Basic peanut butter and jelly. . . . A scoop of vanilla ice cream—a little icy though." She broke off and began to write. "Marlon Brando. B-R-A-N-D-O. Yes."

Casey opened the freezer door and stared at the ice cream carton.

"What's the matter?" her mother asked.

"Nothing." She pulled it out. "It's cold on my fingers."

"A four-letter word for secretary. That's a hard one." Her mother folded the newspaper and put her pencil on top of it. "What is it, Casey? Something's wrong."

Casey reached for a spoon and sat down at the table with the carton in front of her. "How can you tell? You're not even looking at me."

"I don't have to look at you. I know by listening to you. Besides, I'm looking at you now. Where's your spunk today? Is it another sore throat, or something else?"

Casey stared at the ice cream on her spoon, then licked the top. Her mother was right. There were little chunks of ice in it.

She thought back to the day in school. Everybody was acting as if Tracy was the queen of the world.

Catherine had pulled her hair back into braids like Tracy's. She looked like an idiot with two pokey little stalks sticking out behind her ears. And Darlene was saying "really" every two minutes, just the way Tracy did.

Pair of goons.

"Casey?"

"It's Tracy," she said slowly.

"Tracy? I thought you two were such good friends. After we came back from vacation, that was all you talked about, the things you and Tracy had done together, how you wished you could see her again."

Casey held the carton on its side and pretended to

concentrate on getting the last of the ice cream out. "Not much in here."

"What happened?"

She shrugged. "Tracy's different now."

"How different?"

"We have a skit to do for one thing. She wants to do George Washington."

"What's the matter with poor George?"

"Everybody knows about him. Only a dumb kid would want to . . ."

"Doesn't Tracy have trouble reading?" her mother cut in. "You'd have to read a lot to do somebody new. Maybe she's worried about that."

Casey licked her fingers. "Maybe, but it's more than that. She's running around, making everyone laugh, acting like a complete idiot."

"Listen, Casey," her mother said. "Tracy's new. She's probably shy."

"Shy. That's like calling an alligator shy, or a rhinoceros."

Her mother smiled. "Give her a little more time. She'll probably settle down."

"I guess so."

"In the meantime, get your spunk back. You don't have to walk around like a wet dish towel just because Tracy is here."

Casey picked up the carton and dumped it into the basket. Her mother was right. Why let Tracy take over her whole life? Fifth grade was just beginning . . . and maybe she could get her book started one of these days. . . .

"I know what we can do," her mother said. "We'll have a sleep-over. You can invite all the girls and stay up half the night talking. I'll bet that'll smooth everything out."

Casey thought for a moment. Then she began to grin. *"Ma mère,"* she said, "that's a terrific idea. When?"

"Next weekend."

"Too far away. How about during the week?"

Her mother wrinkled her forehead. "If you don't stay up too late . . . maybe."

"Tomorrow?"

Her mother shook her head. "How about Thursday?"

Casey stood up. "I'm going to see the kids at the library right now to do some social studies. I'll invite them all." She swooped down and gave her mother a kiss. "The old fourth-grade celebrity—whoops!—fifth-grade celebrity is back in action."

Just then the back door banged open. It was Van.

"How was junior high?" Casey asked. "Did you have a spectacular day?"

"Stinks," Van said. "I don't know where I'm supposed to be, what I'm supposed to be doing."

Her mother sighed. "I'm really glad you two are so happy."

"I have a pile of homework," Van said. "Spanish. How can I be happy? I'm lost already."

Casey opened the door. "Too bad it isn't French. Walter's grandmother is teaching me some words.

Bonjour and *chaud,* and *froid,* and *champignon.* I love that word: sham peen yon."

"What does it mean?"

Casey grinned. "Mushroom . . . which you are if you keep worrying about everything."

"Good advice." Her mother picked up her pencil. "A four-letter word for secretary," she muttered.

Casey grabbed her purse from the top of her books. "I'll be back later."

Her mother smiled. "Glad you're feeling better."

"Better?" she said, flashing her braces. "*Fantastique,* or whatever they say in French."

She opened the door and raced down the driveway to call for Walter.

12

"Walter!" Casey shouted from the driveway. "Let's get a move on."

She bent over and touched her toes. She'd show Tracy. She'd show everybody. What a celebrity sleep-over she'd have. What a terrific book she'd write.

She bent over again and twirled her arms in circles. Somehow she'd even make Tracy do someone besides George Washington.

"Walter," she shouted again.

His grandmother popped her head out the front door. "Waltair is in the bathroom. He will be only a month."

"A month?"

"No." Mrs. Thorrien wrinkled her forehead. "A minute. Yes, a minute."

Walter ducked around his grandmother. "You don't have to tell the whole world . . ." he began. He stopped when he saw Casey. "Oh, it's you."

"Who did you expect? Sally Ride?"

Walter stretched out his fingers. "Shriveled up like crazy. What an experiment." He looked at her. "You should have gone without me."

"It's all right. I was talking with my mother and Van anyway."

"Wish I could find a decent shoelace," Walter said. He bent down to knot a little piece of lace into his sneaker.

Casey leaned over, too, and dug at a lump of gravel that had worked its way into her sock.

They stood up together.

Walter came up to her forehead.

Quickly Casey ducked down. She pulled in her chin and bent her knees a little.

She'd probably end up being a giant. The tallest kid in the class, always at the back end of the line.

"Waltair," Mrs. Thorrien called. "When are you coming back? When is the water coming out of the tub?"

Walter waved back at her. "Later," he said. "Tonight."

"Try to . . ." Mrs. Thorrien began.

"I will. Don't worry." He turned to Casey. "My luck. My grandmother is the cleanest woman in the world. She can't even stand water in the tub."

"It is not the water," Mrs. Thorrien said. "It is the blue."

"What does she mean?" Casey asked as they started down the street.

"The experiment. Ink." Walter broke off. "Why are you walking like that?"

"Like what?" Casey tried to straighten her legs a little.

"Hunched over like a pretzel."

Casey felt her face get hot. "Maybe I did something to my back. Strained it. But don't worry about that, *mon cher.* Think about the baby."

She looked down the street. Tracy Matson had just turned the corner. "Hey, Walter!" Tracy yelled. "Casey, old rower!"

One of Tracy's braids was undone again. She was wearing old red shorts and a top with a small tear in the sleeve.

"Great news, *ma chère,*" Casey called.

"I have news too," Tracy said. "I took a look at that social studies assignment. What a nuisance that's going to be."

A big nuisance, Casey thought, especially since Tracy probably couldn't read one line of the social studies book.

"I haven't looked at it yet," Walter said.

"It's all about that guy Macko something." Tracy jumped up and tapped the stop sign with her cast.

"Macko?" Walter asked. "Never even heard of him."

"He went to China, or someplace like that. Boring as anything."

Casey started to giggle. "Macko Wacko. You mean Marco Polo."

Tracy took a quick look at Walter. "Marco. That's what I meant to say."

"He's not so boring," Casey said. "I read a terrific book about him. He was born in Europe, but he went to China when he was only a teenager. This was way back in the twelve hundreds."

She shifted to one foot. It was uncomfortable standing with her legs bent. She glanced over at Walter. He still looked a little shorter.

"Anyway, Marco Polo wrote a book about it afterwards," she went on. "People in China had all kinds of stuff that his country didn't even know about." She began to count on her fingers. "Paper money, fireworks, pepper, silk gowns, rubies . . ."

"Listen, are we going to stand here forever?" Walter asked.

"No, let's go," Casey said, and stretched her legs a little.

A few minutes later they opened the door to the library and started for the back table.

Darlene and Catherine were sitting there, paging through a pile of books.

"Listen, Tracy," Casey said, grabbing the back of her shirt. "I want to talk to you about that George Washington business." She ran her tongue over her braces. "Let's do somebody else."

"Who?"

"Someone different. Someone new. Someone— you know—a celebrity-type per—"

"Hey," Tracy cut in. "I thought you had news."

"Come on over here and sit," Catherine called out to them. "I'm dying of boredom. I need one of Tracy's stories."

"I'm on my way," Tracy yelled.

The librarian looked up frowning and watched until Tracy scraped back a chair and slid into it.

Casey took a breath and marched over to the table.

"Great news, everyone. The latest from the old celebrity. We're going to have the absolutely smash-
ingest sleep-over Thursday night."

Catherine looked up. "Where?"

"My house, of course."

"I don't know," Darlene said. "We were going to
go roller-skating. Tracy said they always do that in
High Flats."

Casey glanced over at Tracy. "It's in Tracy's honor,
of course."

"Of course," Tracy said. "We have to go."

"Sounds good," Darlene said. She tapped one of
the books on the table. "Listen, guys. If we're going
to do this report on Marco Polo, let's get going. I've
got to get home soon." She shoved the book toward
Tracy. "Hey, Tracy, take a look at this encyclopedia.
Maybe you could read it to us. We could begin to get
some ideas."

Tracy stared at her for a moment, her cheeks red-
dening. Then she opened the book and paged
through it. "I really know all about him," she said.
"Your worries are over. Let me tell you."

She sat up a little straighter. "Marco Polo went
from Europe to China. He probably took one of those
sailboat things. Anyway, he wrote a book. I can even
tell you what he wrote about. It's on silk gowns and
stuff like that."

"Hey," Walter said suddenly. "What's my grandmother doing here?"

Casey swiveled around. Mrs. Thorrien was hurrying toward them. "The baby," she said. "It is today. It is now."

Walter sighed. "So long," he told everyone. He started toward his grandmother.

Casey scrambled to her feet. "Wait up. I'm coming too."

Behind her, Casey could hear Tracy rustling the pages of her book. "It was about fireworks too. Do you know the people in Europe didn't even know about them when Marco was alive? And pepper. And . . ."

Casey closed the door behind her hard. Already Walter and Mrs. Thorrien were starting up the street. Casey had never seen Walter's grandmother walk so fast.

She rushed after them.

13

An hour later, Casey leaned back against Walter's front steps. She was getting tired of sitting there, tired of waiting. She had spent all that time thinking about Tracy Matson.

She was certainly tired of thinking about Tracy.

How could Tracy have done that? How could she have told all that stuff about Marco Polo . . . made herself look big.

Casey tried to think about her own book. Maybe she could write an adventure. Somewhere in China, maybe . . .

"What a waste of time this is," Walter said, and jumped off the step. "I should be inside, working on my science experiment, instead of hanging around on my front steps."

"What's the experiment anyway?" Casey asked.

"A volcano."

"Didn't we do one of those a while back?"

He sat down again. "Not with blue ink. Not as big as a bathtub."

Casey's eyes widened. "Your grandmother is going to kill you if that explodes all over the ceiling."

"That's why I'm out here. It's much easier to work when she's at the store or something."

"I thought you were waiting for your father to get back from the hospital."

"I forgot about that." He picked at some of the moss growing in between the steps.

"You're joking," Casey said.

"I guess so."

"Aren't you excited? Can't you just picture what it's going to be like to have a baby? A sister or a brother?"

"A sister," he said. "My mother had some kind of test. It's going to be a girl . . . probably some kind of nuisance."

"Yaahoo," a voice screeched from down the block. He looked up. "Who's that?"

Casey gritted her teeth. "Who do you think? Tracy."

Tracy dashed across the lawn and sank down on the bottom step. "Hey, guys, what is it? Girl or boy?"

"We just went through that," Walter said. "She's not born yet."

"Whole thing's going to be a big pain," Tracy said. "A big pain in the bazoo."

"You mean like the assignment on Marco Polo?" Casey said without looking at her.

"Listen, Casey . . ." Tracy began.

"Tracy's right," said Walter. "I'll have diapers in with my socks, pink blankets shedding all over my shirts."

"A pain in the bazoo," Tracy repeated. "Poopsie Pomeranz's mother had a baby last winter. He cries until your ears ring, he spits up all over everybody."

"Whole thing's going to be a big pain," Tracy said.

She held her nose with two fingers. "And smell. Whew! I won't even tell you what he smells like most of the time."

The front door opened. Mrs. Thorrien stuck her head out and handed them two plates. "It is time for the supper." Then she spotted Tracy. "I will bring another plate."

"What is it?" Tracy asked.

"The seafood crepe," Mrs. Thorrien said.

Casey looked down at it and gulped. A grayish sauce oozed out of the crepe.

"Great," Tracy said. "I'll stay. I love fish. It reminds me of High Flats."

"Mmm," Walter said. "The sauce is wonderful." He lifted the crepe out of the sauce and ran his finger around in it. "Delicious."

Casey stared at a pair of black lumps floating in the sauce. She wondered if they were eyes. "Yes," she said, "wonderful."

"I will be back in a week," Mrs. Thorrien told Tracy.

"You mean a minute," Walter said absently.

Casey slid over to the edge of the steps. She could see Walter's cat, Carrots, half asleep behind the bushes. She waved the plate around a little. Carrots ate anything, even spiders.

Walter put half of the crepe in his mouth at once. "You're right, Tracy," he mumbled. "This whole baby business is a pain in the neck."

Tracy picked at the bottom edge of her cast. "Some kids go crazy over babies. Just crazy."

Walter jerked his thumb toward Casey.

"All they want to do," Tracy went on, "is googledy goo. Really."

Casey looked at the cat as hard as she could.

He opened one green eye for a moment, then closed it again.

"Aren't you going to eat that?" Walter asked.

"Of course," Casey said. She cut a piece from the edge and put it into her mouth. It tasted like eels or seaweed.

"I have more important things on my mind than babies," Tracy said.

Walter pushed at his glasses. "So do I."

Casey tore off another piece of the crepe, gave Tracy and Walter a quick look, then tossed it backwards toward the cat.

A moment later she swiveled her head around. The whitish piece of crepe was dangling from the end of the azalea bush.

Mrs. Thorrien stuck her head out the door. "Here," she told Tracy. "I wish Walter's father would come . . . or call."

"Me too." Casey smiled up at her.

Tracy started to eat in big mouthfuls. "Just like home," she said, and sighed a little.

Casey took another tiny bite of the crepe. She wished Tracy were home, back in High Flats where she belonged. She tried to chew without tasting the crepe. She wondered if Mrs. Thorrien could see the azalea bush from the top step.

Tracy glanced over at her. "I'll eat yours."

Casey glared at her. "I like it."

Mrs. Thorrien smiled at Casey. "Some children do not like seafood. Some grown-up people too. I myself did not eat this when I was a girl. Now I am used to it. I like it."

She reached out for Casey's plate. "I have some of the plain crepes inside. I will put a little of the *confiture* on them for you." She patted Casey's shoulder. "You must try just one more taste of the seafood. It will start you on the road to loving it."

Casey took a small forkful of the crepe, avoiding the black lumps. *"Confiture,"* she said, hoping it would be better than the seafood.

"Yes, *confiture*. It is"—Mrs. Thorrien wrinkled her forehead—"Jell-O."

"Jelly," Walter said. "Jam."

"Whew," Casey breathed.

Mrs. Thorrien laughed. "Now," she said, "I will give the food of the sea to the cat. He will think he has arrived in heaven."

Casey took a quick look at the azalea bush. The crepe was gone and Carrots was cleaning his whiskers with an orange paw.

Just then Walter jumped off the step. "Here comes my father."

"Praise be," said Mrs. Thorrien.

Casey looked up. The Moleses' blue Fiero was turning the corner into 200th Street. She stood up and followed Walter down the front path.

Mr. Moles pulled into the driveway. For a moment he sat there grinning at them.

Mrs. Thorrien hurried to the car. "Tell me quickly, is everything all right?"

He opened the car door. "You have a granddaughter." He turned to Walter. "And you have a sister, Gabrielle."

"Oh," Casey said. She beamed at Walter, but he wasn't looking at her. He was staring down at his sneakers.

"What a wonderful day," Mrs. Thorrien said.

Mr. Moles patted her on the shoulder. "It's the day we've been waiting for."

Suddenly Walter took off down the street.

Casey stared after him. "What's the matter?"

"Just going to take a run around the block," he yelled back. "I've been sitting around here too long."

Mrs. Thorrien shook her head. "Come, Casey, I will make you some crepes with the *confiture,* and some for the father too."

Casey followed them up the front path. Tracy was still sitting there, eating the last of her crepe. She stood up. "I'm going for a run with Walt," she said, brushing at her mouth. "I think I'm just the person he'd like to be with right now."

Casey looked back over her shoulder as Mr. Moles held open the front door for her.

"Wait up, Walter," Tracy yelled, halfway down the path.

Casey watched Tracy dash down the street, braids bouncing. Walter leaned against the telephone pole until she caught up with him, then they turned the corner together.

Casey took a deep breath, then she went into the Moleses' kitchen and sat down at the table, half listening as Mrs. Thorrien asked about the baby.

"She is beautiful?" Mrs. Thorrien took a jar of grape jelly out of the closet and spread it onto the crepes.

Mr. Moles winked at Casey. "I think she looks like a pumpkin, but her mother says she looks like an angel."

"Angel Gabrielle," said Mrs. Thorrien.

Mr. Moles smiled. "Yes."

Casey ate her crepe quickly, wondering where Walter and Tracy had gone. Then she pushed her chair back. "I loved the *confiture.*"

Mrs. Thorrien smiled. "You may love the seafood someday."

Casey smiled back, then let herself out the back door and started across the lawn. She hoped they hadn't noticed how quiet she was. She felt as if she were going to cry. It seemed as if Tracy was taking over her whole life, stealing her ideas, her friends. She swallowed. Now even Walter.

She stopped in the middle of the lawn and squared her shoulders, thinking about what her mother had said. She wasn't going to waste one more minute thinking about Tracy Matson.

14

Marcia Terranova was a spy. She had stolen her country's secrets. Now there would be war. But Marcia didn't care. Marcia didn't care about anything. She tossed back her red braids . . .

"Horrible," Casey said aloud. She sat up and shoved the notebook under the bed. *Captured in China* wasn't working out either.

If only she'd hear from Amanda Cornfield, the author. She stood up and went downstairs to the living room. Van was standing on her head in the middle of the rug.

"Would you mind getting out of the way," Casey said. "I'd like to turn on the television."

Van flipped over and ran her hands through her hair. "What a bother you are, Casey."

Casey knelt down and twisted the dial. "How come the whole thing goes up and down all the time? We need a new TV."

Van braced herself and stood on her head again. "Do something else. Go somewhere else."

"Maybe I'll go over to Walter's and see what he's

doing." She went out the front door, crossed the lawn, and rang the Moleses' front bell.

Nobody answered.

She moved back until she could see Walter's window. It was closed tight and the shade was down to the sill. "Walt?" she shouted.

She went back up the steps and leaned against the bell. She could hear it ringing inside. She put her ear against the door to see if she could hear footsteps, but everything was quiet.

She sank down on the top step. Maybe Walter had gone to the hospital with his grandmother to see the baby.

Just then her mother popped her head out the door. "Telephone, Casey."

Casey dashed across the lawn again and opened the door. "Coming." She wondered who'd be calling her. She raced into the kitchen. "Hello," she said a little breathlessly.

It was Walter. "Get over here fast," he yelled. "Help."

"I was just there. No one's home. I rang and rang."

"I'm here. I'm here. Where do you think I'm calling from? Chicago?" He broke off. "Just hurry. Let yourself in."

Casey dashed out the back door, across the yards, and up Walter's back steps. The door was locked.

She circled around to the front and let herself in. "Walt?"

"Up here, for Pete's sake," he yelled down to her.

She ran up the stairs. There was blue water all over the hall floor. "You've got a flood," she said.

"More towels," Walter yelled from the bathroom. "Try the basement. I've used up all the ones in here."

Casey rushed down the stairs. Through the living room window, she spotted someone walking up the street. It looked like Tracy.

Casey ran her tongue over her braces. She didn't want to see Tracy, she didn't even want to think about her. She ducked behind the window and sped down to the laundry room.

It was exactly the same as her mother's. The same throw-up green paint that had been on sale in Mr. Moles's hardware store, the same yellow clothes washer and dryer. But the rest of the room was different. It was clean, immaculate. Not one piece of laundry on the floor or in the basket. No towels anywhere.

She rushed up the stairs again. "No good, Walter."

"Get my bedspread," he said.

"You can't . . ."

"I can so," he said. "My grandmother's thinking about the baby so much she won't even notice."

She raced into his room and took a look at the blue spread on his bed.

It was hideous.

It had about a thousand red cars all over it, and each little car had a driver in black goggles.

She yanked it off the bed, rolled it up into a ball, and tore into the bathroom.

She could feel the water oozing through the hole in

her sneaker, soaking her sock. "Yikes, it's cold," she said.

He looked up. He was sloshing water all over the floor with a sopping wet towel.

"Throw that bedspread right in here," he said. "Nobody will be home for another hour. By then . . ."

Casey dropped the spread on the floor and watched as the water soaked into it.

"The cars are drowning," Walter said.

"So are the drivers with their teeny little goggles."

"Good. About time." Walter stood up. "That's a crummy-looking bedspread. I've had it since I was the baby's age." He started to move the spread around the floor with his foot.

His jeans had big wet patches all over them.

"You're drowning too," Casey said.

"I just hope this doesn't come through on the kitchen ceiling," he said, poking at his glasses.

The front doorbell rang.

Walter looked at her. "That's probably Mrs. Brown or some gabby guts like that. Don't answer."

Tracy, Casey thought.

The front bell kept ringing.

"Good grief," Walter said. "I can't stand that noise. Go into my mother's bedroom and take a look out the window."

Casey walked into Mrs. Moles's room slowly. At the foot of the bed was a cradle. A puffy pink blanket hung over the edge. It was covered with lace.

Casey tiptoed closer. She reached out and touched

the lace with one finger. Beautiful, she thought. She couldn't wait to see the baby.

She went over to the window and peeked out. She could see the top of Tracy's red hair. She jumped back as Tracy looked up.

Tracy leaned on the bell again.

Casey felt like throwing the cradle down on top of her. She pressed her nose against the screen. "Give me a break with that noise," she yelled.

Tracy stepped back. "What are you doing up there?"

"Who is that anyway?" Walter yelled from the bathroom.

"It's Tracy," she said reluctantly.

"Let her in."

"Door's open," Casey called down. She started down the stairs as Tracy opened the front door.

A moment later Walter came into the living room holding the dripping bedspread and towels in his arms.

"You got a Jacuzzi?" Tracy asked, looking up at him.

Walter blinked a little. "I wish I did. What are you doing here?"

"I came to see how your volcano is coming along. If it's any good, I may set one off on Leroy Wilson's front porch when I get back to High Flats. Pa-bahm!"

"When are you going back to High Flats, anyway?" Casey asked.

Tracy looked out the window. "Who knows? Rebel has probably forgotten what I look like by this time."

Walter darted past them. "Got to get this in the washer," he said.

Tracy moved around Casey and plumped herself down in a chair. She twirled one red braid around her finger. "I was just over at Darlene's house."

"Darlene? Did she invite you?"

Tracy raised her shoulder in the air. "I just went. Catherine was there too. They were working on their skit. Michael Jackson, I think. They're trying to keep it a secret." She leaned over and helped herself to a handful of Mrs. Moles's chocolate creams.

Wouldn't you know, Casey thought, Michael Jackson, the singer. A real celebrity. "Listen, Tracy, we've got to work on our skit. Right away. And not George Washington."

Tracy's cheeks were bulging with chocolate. She mumbled something, then stuffed another cream into her mouth.

Walter stamped back into the living room. "I'll just let that spread twirl around in the washer for a while. It was a dumb thing to forget about turning off the faucet again."

He pulled at his T-shirt. A dark wet patch covered the picture of the palm tree on the front. "Turn to Channel Nine, will you, Casey? I think there's some kind of horror show playing. *Frankenstein*, maybe."

Casey started fiddling with the knobs. Walter's set was almost as bad as hers.

"I told Darlene we weren't going to be bothered doing someone like Michael Jackson," Tracy said as she reached for another cream. "Old George Washington is good enough for us."

"Atta girl, Tracy," Walter said. "That's why I'm doing Thomas Jefferson."

"Thomas Jefferson," Casey muttered. "That's just like doing George Washington. That's the whole thing. They're too easy."

"That's the best part," Tracy said. "Listen to your class president. It won't be any work at all."

Casey stood up. "I'm going home now," she said.

" 'Night, Casey," Walter said, staring at the screen.

"See you tomorrow," Tracy said. "Don't forget, two more days until the sleep-over. In my honor, of course."

Casey stamped across the living room floor and turned back to look at Tracy.

Tracy was scooping up the last piece of candy in the dish.

Casey opened her mouth but couldn't think of a thing to say. She banged open the front door and crossed the driveway to her house.

15

On Thursday evening Casey dumped a bag of potato chips into the largest bowl she could find, tucked a can of peanuts under her arm, and raced down the stairs to the basement.

She had spent the entire afternoon fixing it up, dusting old spiderwebs out of the corners, sweeping up the gray tiled floor.

She set the potato chips and peanuts down on a table and rubbed away a little dust from around the lamp. Then she sat down on the old green couch and looked around.

The basement looked perfect. She had tacked up a poster over the stain on the wall, and no one would ever notice the rip on the flowered chair.

Everything was quiet. Her mother and father had gone to get the pizza and Van was studying Spanish in her bedroom.

She wondered where the kids were. They should have been there a half hour ago. Maybe no one was coming. Maybe they had all forgotten.

She stood up on the couch, rubbed at the window, and peered out. It was almost dark. She could just about see Walter's legs on his driveway, and the bush near the front steps, but she couldn't see the street or even the front path. She jumped down and grabbed a potato chip.

Just then the side bell rang. She went to the stairs. "Down here," she yelled as soon as she had swallowed the chip.

Mindy pushed open the door and popped her head in. "Everyone's coming," she said, starting down the stairs. "Tracy and Catherine are right behind me. Darlene's just getting some tapes for us to listen to."

Tapes, Casey thought. Maybe Van would lend them her stereo. She ran her tongue over her braces. Too bad she hadn't known about Darlene's tapes an hour ago, before she had had that bang-up fight with Van over who was going to use the bathroom first.

"Here comes your president," a voice yelled. A purple sleeping bag hurtled through the open door. Tracy scooped it up, pounded down the stairs, and went straight to the jar of peanuts.

Catherine was right behind her, giggling. "That Tracy is a riot, isn't she?"

"My mother's coming with the pizza any minute," Casey said. "Some with pepperoni, some plain just in case . . ."

"Help," Darlene called from outside. "I have about a thousand tapes here."

Casey rushed up the stairs, Tracy right behind her, and took some of the tapes. "Listen, Darlene, we may not be able to listen to this stuff. I mean my sister has the stereo and . . ."

"Come on," Tracy said. "Don't worry about the

stereo. We can talk and eat." She grinned. "I like that just as much."

They went downstairs and plopped down on Mindy's sleeping bag.

"Now," said Tracy, looking around. "What are we going to talk about?"

"Boys," Catherine said.

"Casey's always looking at Gunther Reed," said Darlene.

"Gooney?" Tracy asked, surprised.

"I am not," said Casey. "I certainly am not."

"He's almost as bad as old Leroy Wilson up in High Flats," Tracy said. "Hands full of fish gunk, nose running . . ."

"Gross," Darlene said. "Disgusting. Tell us about him."

Catherine giggled. "Tracy probably likes Leroy."

Tracy slapped the sleeping bag and laughed. "You should have seen him looking at old Casey here. He thought she was gorgeous." She stopped. "Did I tell you about the time I taught Casey to row?"

"Not that again," Casey said, sitting up a little straighter. "I'm getting sick of hearing about that over and over again."

"She took the oars," Tracy began, sticking her tongue out on one side. "This is the face she made."

Everyone started to laugh. "That looks a little like Casey," Catherine said.

Casey could feel her face getting red. "Let's talk about something else."

Tracy stuck her tongue out a little more and began

to pant. "Here's Casey clunking from one side of the river to the other." She made rowing motions with her arms.

Darlene threw herself back on the sleeping bag, laughing hysterically.

"It's not that funny," Casey said.

"It is," said Catherine, leaning against Mindy, giggling.

Casey looked at Tracy. She was acting like a big idiot, still making rowing motions.

Suddenly Casey wanted to lean over and smack her. Worse, she wanted to tell her to go home to High Flats where she belonged. She was sick of Tracy telling stories on her, sick of Tracy grabbing at her friends.

She opened her mouth.

"I'll tell you a story," she said, glaring at Tracy. "Another story about High Flats. About Tracy. But it's not about rowing. It's about a play we tried to put on."

Tracy stopped rowing. "You mean the play we almost did with Leroy and Richard and Bobby."

"Yes." Casey nodded at her. "Remember? First we were going to do an adventure . . ."

Tracy twirled her braids around her head. "Leroy was in a panic because I wanted him to be a tree." She stood up on the blanket and held her arms up in the air. "That was the only thing that dummy could do without messing up."

"But Leroy didn't want to be a tree," Casey cut in. "And Richard didn't want to be a rock."

"Everybody was fighting over what to do." Tracy sank back on the blanket. She looked at Casey. "I don't even remember what happened next. Do you?"

Casey touched her braces for a moment. "Yes. I was going to get a book of plays, remember?"

Suddenly Tracy's face turned red. "I remember Poopsie Pomeranz dancing around . . ." Her voice trailed off.

"And then Richard said it wouldn't be any good to get the book. You know why?"

"I'm starved," Tracy said. "Just dying of hunger. I wonder when your mother's coming back."

"Richard calls Tracy a chickadee," Casey said. "So does Leroy."

"Chickadee?" asked Darlene. "Why?"

"It's the name of a reading group," Casey said. "The slowest reading group in the world. And guess who's in the group?"

"Casey . . ." Tracy began.

"Sure," said Casey. "It's our old class president, Tracy Matson herself."

For a moment no one said anything. Then everyone began to laugh. Casey looked around at them. They thought she was joking. She opened her mouth to say something else.

Then she looked at Tracy. Tracy's face was blotchy, her eyes brimming. She stood up quickly and went to the jar of peanuts.

Casey stared at her back. She could feel a hard knot in the center of her chest. She wondered how she

could have told that on Tracy, how she could have
been so mean.

Just then the side door opened. "Pizza," her
mother called down.

Darlene and Catherine stood up. "Let's go, guys,"
Darlene said. "Come on, Tracy."

Casey waited until everybody had gone up the
stairs. Then she followed them slowly into the
kitchen.

16

Casey finished her science questions, then glanced across the aisle. Tracy was doodling on her cast with a magic marker. She wondered if Tracy was angry about that Chickadee business last night. Probably not. No one had mentioned it for the rest of the night. She felt guilty, though, and uncomfortable.

Up in front Mrs. Eddie cleared her throat. "I have a little surprise. We're going to the auditorium to start to work on some of the skits onstage." She looked down at Casey. "Perhaps Cassandra will share some of her book with us too."

Casey stared down at her desk. "It's at home."

"It's going to be great," Tracy said. "Just great."

The class lined up. In front of her Tracy leaned over. "Suppose she calls on us? We haven't practiced."

Casey closed her eyes for a moment. Then she marched up to the front of the room. She tried to make herself look sick. "I think I've got a virus," she told Mrs. Eddie.

"Again?"

"Casey's stagestruck," said Gunther. "Or is it stage fright?"

Mrs. Eddie frowned again. "Try to hang in during

the skits. If you don't feel any better later, you can go to the nurse."

Casey sighed. She went to the end of the line.

Tracy moved back three places to get in front of her. "You can be George Washington," she said. "I'll be an army guy or something."

Casey looked down at the tiled floor. She wanted to grab one of Tracy's fat red braids and pull as hard as she could. "That's going to be so dumb," she said. "I can't believe you'd want to do something like that."

The line snaked out of the classroom and down the hall to the auditorium.

Casey pushed open the girls' room door as they passed by and went in for a moment. She bent over the sink, scooped some water up in her hands, and took a sip. It tasted like metal.

She went outside again and lagged behind the line as they went into the auditorium.

Maybe if she was last, Mrs. Eddie wouldn't notice her, wouldn't call on them. She watched Tracy prancing along in front of her, talking to Gunther and twirling her braids around.

Casey went into the last row and banged down one of the seats. She slid down into it so the back of her head rested on top of the chair.

Darlene and Catherine were first. Darlene started to sing in a Michael Jackson voice. She was terrific. Catherine was playing the piano.

Casey slid down a little farther in the chair.

Up in front Tracy was pulling a pile of white cotton

out of her purse. She began to twirl it around in her hands.

Casey glanced at Mrs. Eddie. Suppose she called on them.

J. R. Fiddle and Walter were next. Casey could hardly hear what they were saying, something about Thomas Jefferson and the Civil War.

Mrs. Eddie was frowning. "Civil War?" She shook her head. "A little late for Thomas. He was dead by that time . . . for about forty years."

A couple of kids in the front started to laugh. Walter and J.R. didn't seem to care one bit. They jumped off the stage, grinning. Casey guessed they were just glad to have the whole thing over with.

She leaned forward a little to see the big clock on the side wall. Twenty minutes left before they had to go to lunch.

Mrs. Eddie looked around. "How about you?" she asked Mindy and Joanne.

Mindy played the part of Princess Di and Joanne was Queen Elizabeth. They weren't as good as Darlene and Catherine, but they were a hundred times better than Walter and J.R.

Mrs. Eddie tapped her finger against her lip as Mindy and Joanne came down off the stage.

She glanced back at Casey. "Cassandra has a little virus, so maybe we'd better have someone else."

"Virus smirus," Gunther said.

Casey could hear Catherine and Darlene giggle a little.

Mrs. Eddie must have heard them too. She stared

hard at Casey. "I guess you can give it a try, Cassandra. You and Tracy."

Casey walked up the aisle slowly, watching Tracy climb up on the stage, grinning. She could feel her cheeks burning. "We really haven't done much practicing," she told Mrs. Eddie.

Mrs. Eddie tapped her plan book with a pencil. "This assignment was given the first day of school. Who are you working on?"

Casey didn't answer for a moment. She looked up at Tracy.

Tracy's face was a little red too.

"Well, Cassandra?" Mrs. Eddie asked. "Tracy?"

"George Washington, I guess," Tracy said.

"Not too much imagination went into that decision," Mrs. Eddie said.

Casey walked up the three steps to the stage.

She stood there, not knowing what to do with her hands, feeling everyone's eyes on them.

"I have a prop," Tracy said a little uncertainly. "A wig."

Casey looked down at her feet, trying to think of something to say. She cleared her throat. "George Washington is the father of our country," she said at last.

"He was the first president," Tracy added.

Down below everyone was looking at them.

"He won the war for independence," Casey said.

"That's right," said Tracy.

Casey could feel tears behind her eyes. She blinked a little.

"He rowed across the Potomac River," Tracy said. "I think. I don't remember why."

"All right, girls," Mrs. Eddie said. "That's enough of that."

Casey jumped off the stage. She rushed up the aisle pretending not to see Gunther snickering or the rest of the kids looking at her.

She tried to look as sick as she could.

It wasn't hard. She wished she had typhoid, or sleeping sickness. She wished she could walk out the school door and never come back.

She banged open the girls' room door and went inside to stand by the window.

A moment later Tracy came in too. "Are you really sick?" she asked.

Casey stared at her for a moment. "Sick of you," she said slowly.

Tracy stood there, not moving, her eyes on Casey's face. "I thought we were best friends," she said. "Remember last summer?"

"We're not best friends anymore," Casey said. "And I hardly remember last summer."

She watched Tracy's freckled face, trying to see if Tracy really cared.

But Tracy walked over to the sink after a moment and scooped up some water for a drink. She didn't look upset, or worried, or anything. A little water dribbled off her chin.

"Not best friends, not even friends," Casey said, still watching. She felt a sharp touch of anger. Tracy

"Not best friends, not even friends," Casey said.

didn't care one bit that she had changed her whole life around. "Just stay away from me," she said.

"I'll be going home soon anyway," Tracy said, reaching for a paper towel. "Maybe we won't even have to do the skit together."

Casey walked past her. "I hope not. I'd be glad if you went home tomorrow."

She looked over her shoulder at the back of Tracy's hair. One braid was coming out. Tracy was combing it with her fingers. And in the mirror, Casey could see that Tracy's eyes were filled with tears.

17

Casey washed her hands for the third time, then dried them carefully on the towel. She wasn't going to think about the book, or school, or Tracy for the rest of the day.

She sighed. Last night she had dreamed about being in the rowboat with Tracy. She could feel the sun on her face, could hear Tracy laughing.

"Mother," Van yelled, "will you get that kid out of the bathroom?"

Casey banged the door open. "Hold your horses, will you?"

"I thought you drowned yourself," Van said. She pushed past Casey and slammed the bathroom door behind her. "I have no time to wait around. I have homework . . ."

Casey raced down the stairs. "The baby's coming home from the hospital. I'm on my way over to Walter's right now."

Casey's mother frowned a little. "Maybe you shouldn't. Mrs. Moles might be tired. She may want to relax a little."

"I don't think so," Casey said. "I think her feelings might be hurt if I weren't there."

She held out her hands. "I washed about a million

times, just in case. I might get to hold the baby, or give her a bottle or something."

She went out the front door and across the lawn. Mrs. Thorrien was in the kitchen with Walter. *"Une bonne journée,"* she said. "A happy day."

Casey smiled a little, trying to put Tracy out of her mind.

"I have everything ready. I have taken everything out of the bathroom cabinets and put in her little clothes."

"Whole place is being changed around," Walter said.

"We must make room for this new lettle *bébé,"* Mrs. Thorrien said. "This angel. We must make her welcome. Make her comfortable. In the beginning everything will seem strange, but then—poof. It will be as if she always is here."

Casey looked down at the counter. "Hey!"

There was a homemade chocolate cake on a plate in the center. On top, ANGE was written in big white letters.

"Angel in French, right?" Casey asked.

"Angel, angel, that's all I hear," Walter said. "I thought her name was Gabrielle."

"It's a little nickname," Mrs. Thorrien said, "because she is loved."

Walter ran his finger along the edge of the cake plate. "Why did you make that dark chocolate? I like the light better." He licked the top of his finger. "Much better."

"Your mother likes the dark. It is her cake." Mrs.

Thorrien hobbled over to the table and sat down, sighing. "My poor feet." She bent over and rubbed at her shoe. "I have hurt the fingers."

"The fingers?" Casey and Walter looked at each other and grinned.

Mrs. Thorrien nodded. "The fingers of my feet. I fell over the spread of Waltair's bed. It was on the floor in the room of the laundry. With towels. Many towels."

"I forgot about them," Walter said. "I completely forgot."

"But what were they sitting there for?"

"Sitting there?"

"Yes."

"I took them out of the dryer," Walter said, "but then J.R. called."

"You washed the spread?"

Walter nodded.

"He is turning out to be a clean boy after all," Mrs. Thorrien told Casey. "Praise be."

Walter took another dab of icing and pushed the cake plate toward Casey. "Have some, George."

"Not funny." Casey sighed and picked at a small lump of chocolate.

"What are you sighing about? A little skit? So what if it's terrible? I don't care one bit how old Thomas Jefferson comes out."

"Well, I care," Casey said. "Some celebrity I turned out to be." She stopped and looked down at the table. She could feel a lump in her throat.

"Listen, Casey," Walter said. "How would you like

to have my problems—somebody coming in and taking over everything?"

Casey looked up. "That's just what's happening . . ." She broke off. "I think I hear a car. Is that your mother?"

Walter took a last dab of frosting, then went down the hall. "They're getting out of the car."

Casey followed him to the door and watched as Mrs. Moles came up the front steps. Mr. Moles was right behind her, carrying a pink bundle.

Walter's grandmother limped to the steps and took the baby. "I have never thought I would see a girl," she said. She smiled at Walter. "One grandson I had and that was perfect, but now a *jeune fille*. I can't believe it."

Casey could see she was crying. Even Mr. Moles had tears in his eyes.

"Our angel Gabrielle," Mrs. Moles said.

Casey stood on tiptoes to see the baby better. Her pink lace hat was too big. It covered half her forehead, but some of her soft brown hair lay against her cheek. She yawned, a big yawn, then wrinkled up her nose.

"Beautiful," Casey breathed. The baby lifted one hand. It looked like a tiny starfish.

"I think the baby resembles you," Mrs. Thorrien told Walter's father.

Casey stared at the baby.

She didn't look one bit like Mr. Moles. Mr. Moles had a huge nose.

Walter's mother must have known what she was

thinking. She grinned at Casey and took the baby from Mr. Moles. "I'm going to put her in her crib," she said. "I'll be right down."

Casey followed Walter and Mrs. Thorrien to the kitchen.

She was dying to hold the baby. She had been holding her breath, hoping that Mrs. Moles would ask her.

"Casey! Walter!" Mrs. Moles called from upstairs. "Come on up. Maybe you want to hold Angel for a minute or two."

"I'll do it some other time," Walter said.

Casey dashed up the stairs. She rubbed her hands on the sides of her jeans. Then she sat down on the pale green puff of a chair next to Mrs. Moles's bed and held out her arms.

Mrs. Moles settled the baby on Casey's lap. "She's so new. It's hard to imagine that she'll be like you in a few years."

Casey looked down at her. The baby's mouth was open, and Casey could see her tiny pink tongue moving.

"She must be dreaming about something to drink," Mrs. Moles said, smiling.

Casey curved her arm a little tighter around the pink bundle. The baby felt warm, and smelled sweet.

"Let's go, Casey," Walter said.

She looked up. Walter stood in the doorway. He had a rim of chocolate around his mouth.

"Here," said his mother. "Wouldn't you like to hold the baby?"

Casey looked down at the baby.

Walter shook his head. He walked into the room, over to Casey, and looked down at the baby.

Casey wondered what he was thinking. Then she realized what was wrong. Walter had been grumpy all this time about the baby. How could that be? She touched the baby's soft cheek with one finger.

"Let's go," Walter told Casey again.

Mrs. Moles took the baby from her. "You have a way with babies," she said. "She's fallen asleep."

Walter peered over his mother's shoulder. "I guess I'll hold her later. Let's go downstairs."

Casey followed him into the kitchen.

"Time for cake," Mrs. Thorrien said.

Walter went out the back door. "I'll wait for you outside."

Mrs. Thorrien cut Casey a big slice and motioned her to the table.

Casey slid into the chair and took a bite. "Delicious."

Mrs. Thorrien beamed at her. "It is the favorite of my daughter."

"The baby is wonderful," Casey said. "I can't understand why Walter doesn't like babies." She stabbed the cake again. "Maybe because he's a boy?"

Mrs. Thorrien sat down at the table across from her. "No, it is not that, Casey. Boys like babies as well as girls. It is this baby. Gabrielle. Angel."

Casey opened her mouth. "But she's beautiful. I'd love . . ."

Mrs. Thorrien shook her head. "It is like the seafood crepes." She bent over and rubbed at her foot. "It is hard to have something different in your life."

"Walter . . ."

"Waltair feels that Angel will steal a little of his place. He thinks things will not be the same anymore."

"But they will be," Casey said. She took a last bite of cake.

Mrs. Thorrien shook her head. "No, Casey. They will not be the same. The family is changed. Waltair has to give up some things. It is hard for him."

Walter popped his head in the back door. "Are you going to take forever in there?"

"I'm coming," Casey said. "This minute." She stood up.

Walter banged the door shut. She could hear him slapping a ball against the back step.

She looked at Mrs. Thorrien. "I never thought of that."

Mrs. Thorrien smiled. "But the giving up is only one part. The other part is the getting."

"He'll have the baby now."

"Yes, another person to love, a person to love him."

Casey nodded and wiped her mouth, then she went out the back door.

Walter looked up at her and grinned. "Talk, talk, talk."

She grabbed the ball and bounced it at him. Out of the corner of her eye she saw Tracy Matson turning the corner. She felt an odd little catch in her throat. Tracy was coming to make up. She started to raise her arm to wave at her, but just then Walter threw the ball.

"Missed," he shouted, as she raced for it.

When she looked up again, she saw that Tracy had passed her house.

"Hey, Walt," Tracy yelled. "How about we go for a run?"

Then she spotted Casey. She hesitated for a moment.

Casey swallowed. Tracy wasn't looking for her. Of course not. And she wasn't looking for Tracy either. "I'm going home now," she told Walter. She crossed the lawn, feeling the leaves crumble under her feet.

"Wait a minute," Walter said.

"Can't," she said, feeling that catch in her throat again. She hurried up the driveway and into the house.

18

It was Saturday at last. Casey curled her toes under the blanket and stretched. Maybe she and Walter could work on his experiment together.

She was dying to see the baby again. She could picture her in a pretty pink dress, sleeping in the pink cradle.

Van stirred in the other bed and muttered something.

Then Casey remembered. Tracy. She felt a hard knot in her chest.

Things would have been so different if Tracy hadn't come here. They'd be writing back and forth, she might even be inviting Tracy for Thanksgiving vacation, or Christmas.

She turned over, trying not to think about Tracy's freckled face and the tears in her eyes in the girls' room mirror.

She punched her pillow and sat up.

"Do you have to keep moving around, making all that noise?" Van mumbled.

"Don't worry. I'm getting up right now. I'm going to spend the day at Walter's. I want to see the baby and maybe get to work on an experiment."

"Make a muzzle. You need one."

Casey slid her legs over the side of the bed and threw on a sweatshirt and a pair of jeans. She pushed her feet into her sneakers and went downstairs without tying the laces.

Her mother was in the kitchen drinking a cup of tea and reading a cook book.

She waved her hand at Casey. "Saturday. A beautiful day. I'm in the mood for some serious cooking."

Casey grabbed a piece of bread, tucked an orange in her pocket, and gave her mother a kiss. "Mind if I go over to Walter's?"

"Shrimp creole and pecan tassies, maybe," her mother said absently.

"I hate creole and can't stand pecans," Casey said.

"You're not going to be too happy with dinner, then," her mother said. "And yes, I do mind if you go to Walter's with your breakfast in your hand."

Casey pulled out a chair and began to peel her orange. She hoped she'd get a chance to work on Walter's experiment.

She felt like making a volcano.

She'd like to blow up the whole backyard.

She finished the orange, stuck half the bread in her mouth, and went out the back door.

"Maybe chicken instead of the shrimp," her mother said. "A lot cheaper."

"How come we have chicken every other meal?" Casey asked. "I'm going to cluck any day now."

She didn't wait for her mother to answer. Instead she started across the lawn. She turned back before she reached the driveway and poked her head in the door again.

"Sorry, Mom."

Her mother looked up and grinned. "Some days are like that . . . sit-down breakfasts . . . chicken and pecans."

Casey smiled back.

A moment later she was at Walter's back door, feeling a little better.

If only Tracy Matson didn't keep appearing in her mind like magic, sliding down the rocks near the bridge, or teaching her how to row.

She shook her head and knocked on the back door.

"Come in," Mrs. Moles yelled.

Casey looked around. Usually the Moleses' kitchen was perfect. Today it was a mess, worse than her house. Much worse.

"Here," Mrs. Moles said. "Take this baby for one minute."

The baby's face was red, her mouth open; she was screaming.

Casey sat down at the table and held out her arms. Gently Mrs. Moles handed her the crying baby.

She was damp and wiggly.

Walter walked into the kitchen. "Some mess," he said. "Where's Gram?"

"Downstairs," said Mrs. Moles. She reached for the Pampers box. "Doing wash. I don't remember all this upheaval when you were born."

Walter walked over to Casey and grinned a little.

"Your jeans are wet," he said, trying to speak over the baby's crying.

"Pat her back a little," Mrs. Moles told Casey.

The teakettle started to screech. "And Walter, turn that kettle off," Mrs. Moles said. "I think I'll have to forget about breakfast for a while."

"Give me the baby," Walter said. "Let me try."

Gently he picked her up. "She's a mess too," he said. He sat down on the chair opposite Casey and held the baby up to his chest.

A moment later the baby burped. It was a loud sound, startling Casey and Mrs. Moles. Walter just laughed. "I think she just spit up all over my shirt." He jiggled her a little.

"I think she's stopping," Casey said. "She isn't as loud as she was a minute ago."

"I've got the magic touch," Walter said as she burped again. "She did the same thing last night. Kept everyone up screeching all over the place. My mother tried to get her to be quiet, so did my father. When I held her, Wham-o! She stopped crying and went to sleep." He looked down at her. "Ridiculous for a little thing like this to have a long name like Gabrielle. Maybe I'll call her Angel after all."

Mrs. Moles looked at Casey and winked.

Just then Mrs. Thorrien puffed up from the laundry room. "This baby has made the house turn over," she told Casey. "We have done three wash loads this morning and there is still a pile of her sheets on the floor." She shook her head, smiling.

"All right," Mrs. Moles said. She took the baby. "I can manage now. Thank you both."

Walter looked down at his shirt. "Smells a little. I guess I'll have to get used to it." He stood up. "Listen, Mom. Casey and I want to work in the bathroom. It'll be a little messy."

Mrs. Moles threw her head back and laughed. "That's the least of my worries at this point," she said. "The very least."

Casey followed Walter up to the bathroom.

"Now, here's the experiment." He pointed to a row of things on the bathroom floor.

"Small glass bottle, cork, couple of glass tubes." He held up another bottle. "Ink, of course. Blue-black."

"How did that go again?" Casey asked, sitting on the edge of the tub.

"It's like this. Pour some ink into the little bottle. Add hot water. Slap the cork on top with two tubes in it."

"Then what?" Casey asked.

"Then you're supposed to put the bottle in a larger jar filled with very cold water. Only instead of a jar, I'm using the tub." He tipped the bottle of ink and began to pour it into the small bottle. A little river of ink ran down the side and dripped onto the floor. He rubbed at it with his sneaker.

"One thing about having a baby in the house," he said. "Nobody notices a little ink." He wiped his hands on his shirt. "Nobody notices anything. It's kind of neat."

Casey took the bottle from him and filled it carefully with hot water.

"Now for the best part," he said. "Yahoo! The tub. This time I'm going to remember to turn the faucet off."

He turned on the cold water full blast and leaned over the tub to watch. "Too bad Tracy Matson isn't here. She'd love something like this."

Casey didn't answer. She handed him the small bottle and watched him set it on the bottom of the tub.

"Here we go," he said. "Krakatoa."

"Krak-a-what?"

"That's where they had an underwater volcano like this, a long time ago. I saw a movie about it on TV."

They watched as a cloud of blue suddenly rose from the bottle.

"It works," Walter said. "Look at that. The whole bathtub is going to be blue."

Casey kept watching as the blue water swirled around the tub, coloring it.

Just then Mrs. Thorrien stuck her head in the open doorway. *"Sacré bleu,"* she said as she saw the tub. "This house is a deesaster."

Walter sat back on his heels. "I guess Angel will want to know all about this stuff when she gets big enough."

Casey nodded. She raised her eyebrows. "Nice to have a sister."

Walter leaned over the tub. "I don't know. I didn't

think she'd be so puny, or something. Kind of defenseless. Maybe it won't be as bad as I thought."

He put his hand in the tub. "Let's see if it turns blue."

"Your hand?"

"Certainly." He lifted it out. "Kind of blue at that." He looked at her over his shoulder. "Want to get Tracy? Do the whole experiment over again?"

Casey stared down at the blue water and shook her head. "No, thanks."

"What's the matter with you two anyway? Tracy's a great kid."

"Sure."

"Is it because she's class president?" he asked, leaning over to swirl the water around.

"Of course not," Casey said, her mouth suddenly dry. "Well, a little bit maybe. She really took over everything."

"She said this was the first time she was ever elected class president."

Suddenly Casey thought about Leroy and Richard teasing Tracy. She thought about Tracy saying she hated school. She looked down at the flecks of blue water around the edge of the tub. If only she hadn't told everyone the chickadee story.

Walter pushed the plunger, and a whirlpool of water started to gurgle out of the tub. "Tracy thinks you're pretty smart, writing a book and all that."

Casey sighed. "I'm never going to get to write that book. I don't have one thing to write about. Not one thing."

"Casey," a voice called.

"My mother." Casey stood up. "Got to go, I guess. Maybe the store."

She went down the stairs and peeked into the kitchen. Mrs. Moles was sitting at the table, eyes closed.

Casey went out the back door, thinking about Tracy. She had probably been thrilled when she made class president for the first time, glad that nobody knew she could hardly read or spell.

Just then Van barreled out of the house. She almost knocked Casey over. "Sorry," she said, out of breath. "There's a football game at the junior high. I'm on my way over there right now. There are tryouts for cheerleaders too. I'm going to try for . . ." Her voice faded as she raced down the driveway and across the street.

Casey stared after her. Then she opened the back door. The kitchen was full of steam. Her mother was standing in front of the stove, smiling.

"You look happy," Casey said.

Her mother nodded. "Van just told me she's crazy about school. She just met a boy named Steven. She's made two new girlfriends. She—" She broke off. "No tomatoes. I can't make creole without a can of stewed tomatoes."

"You could try," Casey said.

"Be a good kid," her mother said. "Run down to the store."

Casey took the money her mother held out to her, opened the back door, and started down the driveway. She began to remember Tracy and the ten-cent store and the soda they had never had together.

It was too late now, they'd never have soda together. After Tracy went home, they'd probably never even write to each other again.

19

Casey walked slowly toward Hollis Avenue. The sun was not nearly as strong as it had been a week or so ago. It was getting cold.

She hated to walk all the way up to the avenue. Besides, she'd have to pass Tracy's.

Maybe she should take a little detour. She could walk down 205th Street and angle her way back again.

That was silly.

She squared her shoulders and marched up 204th Street. As she passed Tracy's apartment house she kept her eyes straight ahead. She waited to glance back until she had reached the last house on the block.

Tracy was nowhere in sight. She was probably over at Darlene's or Catherine's, having a wonderful time.

Casey continued on toward Hollis Avenue and turned in at the A&P, trying to remember what her mother wanted from the store.

She spotted Gunther coming toward her, balancing four rolls of toilet paper in his arms. When he saw her he spread his hands, trying to hide the rolls.

Casey grinned at him. "That's a lot of toilet paper."

He turned beet red, then scurried down the aisle away from her.

Casey shook her head, still smiling. Poor Gooney probably didn't want her to know they used toilet paper in his house. She started down the next aisle looking at the cans stacked in neat piles on the shelves. She bumped into Tracy Matson.

Tracy dropped a couple of cans of corn on the floor. They stood there looking at each other for a moment, then they bent down to pick them up.

"Second time this happened in three and a half minutes," Tracy said, not quite looking at Casey. "Gunther Reed is lurking around the place trying to get to the checkout counter without being seen. He's ashamed of buying toilet paper."

Casey felt herself smiling a little. She tried to think of something to say.

"I have to go now, I guess," Tracy said.

Casey nodded. She watched Tracy walking down the aisle, one of her braids undone, a rip in the leg of her jeans.

Then she turned back to the stacks of vegetables. Creole, she told herself, yuck. She saw a stack of stewed tomatoes on the top shelf and reached up for a can. She wouldn't get used to creole for a thousand years. She stood there holding the can in her hand, thinking about Walter getting used to the baby.

Then she began to remember the boat, and Tracy, and talking about stuffing rotten tomatoes in Leroy's sneakers. She almost wished she and Tracy were out on the river today.

Casey bumped into Tracy Matson.

She dusted off the top of the can with one finger. Some of the stuff that had happened the last two weeks wasn't Tracy's fault. It certainly wasn't Tracy's fault that she couldn't write a book. She had made that mess all by herself. And Tracy had only been trying to be nice telling the teacher about it.

It wasn't Tracy's fault that she was class president. She swallowed. And it wasn't even Tracy's fault that all the kids liked her.

The trouble was, Casey thought, she was jealous of Tracy, worried that she was going to take over everything . . . just the way Walter had been worried about Angel.

She hurried back up the aisle to the checkout counter. Maybe she had to get used to Tracy, like the seafood crepes.

Gunther Reed was ahead of her, paying for his toilet paper, but Tracy was gone.

"Hi, Gunther," she said, switching the tomato can from one hand to the other.

He mumbled something, took the bag with the toilet paper, and darted out the door.

"I don't need a bag," she told the checker, handing him the money. "I'm kind of in a hurry."

She slid out the door behind Gooney and looked around.

"Did you see Tracy?" she called after him.

"Nuh-uh," he said without turning around, then he started to run. He disappeared around the corner of 203rd Street.

Casey thought about hurrying, thought about catching up with Tracy.

But what would she say?

She could say she was sorry about the night of the sleep-over, and the other day in the girls' room. She could say that maybe she had to get used to someone being in the classroom, being friends with her friends. She gulped. She could say that she had to get used to someone getting to be class president instead of her.

Just then Tracy popped out from behind the hedges in front of the corner house. She waited for Casey to catch up. "I wanted to tell you—"

"Me too," Casey said. "I want to tell you—"

They looked at each other.

"I should have nominated you," Tracy said. "But it was so exciting to be class president . . ."

"A fifth-grade celebrity," Casey said.

"You were writing that book," Tracy said, "and I can't even read."

"Tracy, I'm so sorry about that night. I . . ."

Tracy held up her hand. "It's alright. Really. About being president. . . . It was all because of Leroy and Richard. I couldn't wait to tell them I was president."

Casey nodded. "About that book." She broke off. "Is someone calling me?" She shaded her eyes. "It's Walter."

Tracy bit her lip. "My being president wasn't exactly . . . I mean . . . Catherine and Darlene were running too. Half the girls voted for Catherine, half voted for Darlene." She sighed. "The boys voted for me because I won an arm-wrestle match with Gunther Reed."

"Casey," Walter yelled from down the street.

"It was the cast," Tracy said. "It kept my arm straight."

Casey grinned. "You became president because you broke your arm?"

"Really," Tracy said. "I was ashamed to tell you before. I wanted you to think I was a celebrity kid like you. You know?"

"Oh, Tracy . . ." Casey began.

Just then Walter pounded up to them. "Come on home. You've got a letter. Your mother said . . ."

Casey wrinkled up her forehead. "A letter?"

"From the famous author," Walter said.

Casey grinned at them. "Just the thing I've been waiting for. Let's go."

They tore down the street to Casey's house and rushed in the side door. The letter was propped up on the kitchen counter.

"Sit down, *mes chers*," she said, waving her hand. "I'll read it aloud."

"Good," her mother said, grinning. "I'll listen while I start the best creole you ever tasted."

Walter and Tracy sat down at the kitchen table as Casey opened the letter. "Listen to this," she said.

"Dear Cassandra,

"Thank you for your lovely letter. I am happy to hear that you want to write a book.

"Here is my advice. Don't set out to write a horrible, scary, exciting, etc., book.

"Write about something or someone you know.

"Let me know how it is coming.

                              "Best wishes,

                              "Amanda L. Cornfield

"P.S. I think I remember you. You had bangs and braces, right?"

"That's it?" Tracy asked. "Write about just any old person you know?"

"That's it," Casey said.

"Sounds like good advice," said her mother.

"Hey," Walter said. "Is that the baby screaming again? She's got some lungs. She's probably dying for her big brother." He stood up and went out the back door.

Casey looked up at the ceiling. "Someone I know about? I'll have to give that a little thought."

Her mother drew in her breath. "Casey, you won't believe this. I don't have any basil."

"Basil?"

"I can't make my famous creole without basil."

Casey looked at Tracy. "I guess we have to go to the store again. Maybe we could talk about that skit too," she said, feeling a knot of worry. "I think it's next week."

"Teamwork, old rower," Tracy said. "We'll think of something."

20

"I hope this works," Casey whispered to Tracy a week later. She pulled the white wig down over her ears. Tracy was wearing her mother's long brown bathrobe. A white cap was perched on her head.

Tracy grinned. "It will. You have the best imagination of anyone I know."

On the stage Walter and J.R. were going on about Thomas Jefferson. J.R. was writing in the air. "It's a declaration of independence," he said in a voice Casey could just about hear.

A moment later, the boys raced off the stage. The audience was clapping halfheartedly.

"Our turn," Casey said. She and Tracy marched to the middle of the stage. The auditorium was packed. Everyone in the school was there.

Casey took a deep breath. "Hand me the oars, Martha," she said in a loud voice. "We're going to row across the river and settle those British nerds once and for all."

"Just like you settled your father's buggy old cherry tree," Tracy said. "Right, George?"

For a moment the audience was silent. Then everyone started to laugh.

Casey pushed at her wig. She grinned a little at Tracy.

"I hope when this war for independence is over," Tracy said in a screechy voice, "everything will calm down. I hope you get a job."

Casey looked up at the ceiling. "I'm sick of being a farmer, Martha. Tired of being a surveyor. What else can I do?"

"Maybe you could get a sit-down job at a desk," Tracy said. She straightened her robe a little.

"Good idea," Casey said. "Maybe I could be president." Casey glanced toward the side of the stage. All the fifth-graders were leaning against the wall, smiling. Mrs. Eddie was nodding her head.

"Terrific, George," Tracy said. "Let's buy a house too. I've always wanted one. Red brick."

"I've got a better idea," Casey said. "We'll get a big white one with columns."

"Nice," said Tracy. "We can call it that. The White House."

"Plain, but okay," Casey said.

The kids in the audience were laughing again. She made believe she was rowing across the Potomac River until they calmed down. She and Tracy went back and forth joking about Washington as president and Martha cleaning the White House. At the end Martha gave George a red plaid suitcase to deliver the farewell address.

They bowed to a thunder of applause. "Celebrity," Tracy whispered as Casey stepped forward.

Casey could feel her hands trembling a little,

"Celebrity," Tracy whispered.

maybe from excitement, maybe from nervousness. "I hope you liked our skit," she said. "I've also written a book—well, a short book—on how George might feel if he dropped in on fifth grade today. I got the idea from Amanda Cornfield, the author. She said to write about what you know." She raised one shoulder. "I certainly know about George."

There was a ripple of laughter. "I know about fifth grade too."

Tracy stepped forward too. "Mrs. Eddie photocopied Casey's book and the class helped staple it together. We're going to give it out later. Read all about it." She grinned. "Martha would love it."

Gooney closed the curtains as everyone started to clap again. Casey and Tracy looked at each other.

"Last day," Tracy said.

Casey reached out and straightened Tracy's white hat. "Don't talk about it," she said. "We still have another hour or so."

Just then Mrs. Eddie came up to them. "You worked together beautifully. Terrific teamwork."

In back of her, Gooney waggled his fingers at her. Mrs. Eddie turned around. "Time for refreshments, everyone. Soda and doughnuts in the cafeteria."

Casey slid into line in front of Tracy. Walter marched along next to her, yawning. "Glad that's over," he said. "I've had enough of Thomas Jefferson to last me for a while."

"You were great," Casey said, fingers crossed in back of her.

Walter grinned. "Well, I wouldn't say great exactly. What do you expect from someone who was up half the night? The only time Angel stops crying is when I hold her."

"That's nice," Casey said. "She knows you already."

In back of her, Tracy gave her a poke. "You never even signed my cast," she said.

Casey reached into her pocket. "I've got a red magic marker right here. I'm going to sign my name twice as big as Leroy Wilson signed his."

21

To Tracy Matson, Fifth-Grade Celebrity:

Start hammering the stand again. George Washington was just the beginning. I've thought of another book to write.

It's all about this kid—I think I'll call her Cassandra Valley. Her best friend comes to town—call her Thérèse Van Matson. Anyway, Cassandra gets kind of jealous because everyone likes Thérèse. She has to get used to her, you know? In the end . . . well I won't tell you that part. You'll have to read the book.

I really miss you, Tracy. I'm so glad you're going to come for the Thanksgiving weekend. We'll have a slam-bang time.

Love from another celebrity,
Casey